YEAR ONE

BLOODSHED ACADEMY

JEN L. GREY

Copyright © 2020 by Jen L. Grey

All rights reserved.

No part of this book may be reproduced in any form or by any electronic or mechanical means, including information storage and retrieval systems, without written permission from the author, except for the use of brief quotations in a book review.

 Created with Vellum

CHAPTER ONE

Today wasn't anything special. It was the same damn thing I had to relive over and over again. If only they knew what I hid inside... There was no way that anyone could ever know though.

I pushed my wolf harder, letting her take control. Times like these were my bliss, but it was rare that I could sneak away to run by myself. Birds chirped above in the trees, and even though it was the end of spring, the grass smelled like rain. These small stolen moments were the only thing that kept my sanity.

Hey, Rave, where are you? Greg's raspy voice appeared in my head.

Great, that lasted all of five minutes. My wolf growled as I pushed her back, letting my human side maintain more control. *Sorry, babe. I thought I heard something and wanted to check it out.*

And you didn't wait for me? A few leaves crumbled under his footsteps as he ran in my direction. *You should know better than to shift this close to school and put yourself in harm's way. Besides, that's my job.*

Sometimes I'd bend the rules when there was a chance I could run wild all on my own. When I could let her out and just be what my wolf wanted us to be. *You're right, but none of the humans saw me change. I made sure of it.*

Oh, come on. Greg appeared as he stepped through the trees with both his and my backpacks slung over his shoulder. He dropped my dark pink bag on the ground and pulled out my track uniform. *Put this on. We're both going to be late for practice.*

I hated being told what to do. That was just one more reason why I didn't belong here; not that it mattered. My wolf snapped at me as I willed her back in. It worried me because each year, she seemed to be getting stronger.

Mustering all my control, I forced my wolf to stand down, and I shifted back to two legs. It didn't take long for it to happen, and of course, I found myself buck naked in front of Greg.

A huge grin filled his boyish face, and he dropped his black bag as he took a few steps toward me. "Damn, you're fine." He wrapped his arms around my waist, resting the palms of his hands on my ass cheeks.

"Greg, stop." I should've known better than to shift in front of him. I purposely avoided situations like these because he'd get pushy. "Someone might see us."

"Oh, come on." His dark brown eyes found mine, and he grabbed my ass. "You know that it's been forever since you've given me any, and it's way past time." His lips landed on mine, and he forced his tongue into my mouth.

How I wished I could think this was romantic, but no... it felt like a slug dancing inside my mouth. It was juicy, limp, and somehow cold. I placed my hands on his chest and pushed him backward. "Though that may be true, now isn't the time or the place. Remember we're going to be late to practice." I grabbed my clothes that had fallen on the ground and quickly dressed before he decided to try again.

"If it wasn't for the big game, I'd be taking you right now." He sighed as he ran his fingers through his short, brown hair. "Come on, we can't be late." He grabbed our bags and then reached for my hand, rushing back through the few trees that had hidden us from the outside, human world.

Ever the obedient girlfriend, I followed behind my alpha, obeying his every command. It made me sick, and my wolf howled loudly in my ears. But this was my role. Women weren't alphas; betas at most, and even that was rare.

As we stepped out into the student parking lot, a group from our pack was standing there, directly facing us. We normally tried not to stand out, but it was hard, especially when we were in a group.

What the hell are you doing? Greg linked the others in, rage evident in his eyes.

Shit, I'd messed up this time.

Darren cringed and glanced down at the asphalt. He ran his hand through his shaggy, black hair and kicked his red baseball cleats on the ground. *Sorry, man. You took off, and we thought there might be a problem.*

What did you expect? Ian lifted his chin as his light green eyes glared at me. *Figured princess was causing trouble.*

That one had never liked me, and I couldn't blame him. One day, he cornered me at school and told me that I wasn't worthy of Greg. That may have been true, but I thought it was more likely that Ian was the only one who could sense my wolf inside and worried my ranking could be higher than his. He was Greg's beta, and it was easy to tell just by looking at him. He was built like a freaking Ford truck and one of the best football and baseball players that Montgomery Central High School had ever seen.

"Oh, don't give Raven a hard time." Sheila tossed her dirty blonde hair over her shoulder and stuck out her boobs that had Indians written across them.

Ugh, I'd always hated the mascot; Indians. I guess that's what you got for living on the outskirts of Clarksville, Tennessee and attending the infamous school that was built on some man-made lake.

"Come on, let's go before the coach throws a fit." Greg ignored Sheila's advances and wrapped an arm around my shoulders. "Dad told me that there might be a scout coming from Bloodshed Academy tonight for the big game. It's the last big one before graduation."

My blood felt as though it turned ice cold, and my wolf perked up at the name. Bloodshed Academy was the elite paranormal school where only the best alphas attended and even fewer graduated. If you weren't there by invitation, wards prevented you from entering—that was just how damn exclusive it was.

"Are you fucking with me?" Ian stopped moving, and his mouth dropped open.

"They're coming here?" Darren's voice cracked, and he smiled like a kid on Christmas morning.

"Hell, yeah!" Greg glanced at my face and moved his hand down my waist possessively. "They called my dad last night and said they were coming to scope me out. What do you think of that, baby?"

Honestly, it bothered me that everything got handed to these four entitled asses. "That's ... great." I tried to put enthusiasm into my words, but they only fell flat.

"Don't sound so happy for him." Sheila faked a frown

while shaking her head. "It's not like it's a big deal or anything."

She was as dumb as a box of bricks, so I must have fumbled worse than I had thought. "No, I am." Even then, my words fell flat. I had to recover and fast. "Sorry, I just have my final exam in Calculus. I'm stressed." I stopped walking and grabbed Greg's arm. As he turned around toward me, I stood on my tiptoes and kissed his lips. "I'm really happy for you."

A wide smile spread across his face, and he bent down for a longer kiss. "You should be happy for us. There's no telling where this will take me."

That was the problem. It was always about where he was going, and my future never seemed to matter. "I can't wait." Somehow, I managed to force those words out and believably too.

"Come on, man." Ian wrinkled his nose and punched Greg in the shoulder. "We're going to be late."

"Yeah, you're right." Greg leaned in and kissed my forehead. "See you at the game, alright?"

"Of course." Ever the doting girlfriend, I had to be there.

The three of them walked off laughing while Sheila, my frenemy, stayed right next to me.

"Do you even care for him?" Sheila narrowed her ice-blue eyes at me.

The truth was that I did care for him. Well I mean, I didn't want him to get bitten by a vampire or anything. So that had to count for something. "Of course, I do. School is just wearing me out."

"I told you that you were crazy for taking on that load." She arched an eyebrow and lifted both hands in the air. "I mean, why do that to yourself? You should have taken it easy. It's not like you're going off to college or anything."

Of all things, she had to bring up that sore topic. "I mean if Greg goes to Bloodshed ..."

"Do you really think you could get in?" Sheila laughed so hard she bent over holding her stomach.

My wolf growled in my head. "No, I thought maybe I'd be able to go to a college too."

"Oh, come on, Raven." Sheila rolled her eyes and began heading toward the track. "We don't go off to college. Bloodshed is the only exception. You'll be heading to community college just like me."

Pressure began to build in my chest, and it almost felt like I might explode. "But if Greg says ..."

"So glad the two of you could show up." Mrs. Smith scowled at the two of us. "It's not like you're five minutes late or anything."

"Sorry, coach." I had to think of something to get us out of trouble.

"Yeah, sorry. Raven couldn't find her shoes so we had to search for Greg to check in his truck." Sheila side-eyed me and sighed. "And of course, that's where they were."

It only seemed fair for her to blame me since my seconds of stolen freedom got us in this predicament. "I was studying on the way to school this morning and must have forgotten to put them in my bag."

"Well, don't let it happen again." Mrs. Smith waved her hand to the left and pointed in the direction of the other runners. "Go catch up to them and warm up. We'll be doing sprints soon."

I took off in a run with Sheila right behind me.

As I entered the house, I found both of my parents in the kitchen.

Mom's dark brown hair was pulled up into a messy bun, and her blue t-shirt had flour dusting the front. "Hey, honey. I'm glad you're home." She opened the oven and pulled out some raw steaks.

Dad wrinkled his nose and fanned his hand in front of his face. "You smell disgusting." Despite his complaining, there was a twinkle in his dark brown eyes.

"I'm sure you wouldn't smell much better after sprinting a total of five miles." My legs still felt like jelly when I walked. It didn't help that my hair was stuck to the back of my neck and my stomach was completely empty. "I'm going to run upstairs and take a quick shower."

"Hurry, we can't be late to Greg's game tonight," Dad called out after me.

Yes, heaven forbid we be late for something of Greg's. Sometimes I wish my parents weren't as tight with Greg's parents. Both sets were bound and determined that he and I were meant to be together. I'd been dating him since I was sixteen in the middle of my sophomore year. Now, here we were seniors and eighteen.

I remembered the night I turned sixteen. Right before I went out on my first date, which had been with Greg, my mom gave me a crescent moon necklace. She had made me promise to never take it off. It was long enough so that even when I shifted, it still stayed around my neck. I'd never taken it off except for one time—last week. The chain broke when I was changing for school, and I had to find a replacement chain. Mom found me and practically lost her shit. She ran into her room, brought me one of hers, and told me to put it back on immediately.

It only took a few minutes for me to bathe, and I felt like

a new human being. As I headed downstairs, there was a knock on the door. Greg's scent hit me before I even reached the door and put me on edge. Why the hell was he here?

Not wasting a moment, I yanked open the door and found him in a clean Indian's baseball uniform. He winked at me and leaned down to kiss me on the cheek. "I see you're wearing the sundress I like."

It almost made me completely regret the decision, but I knew it would be hell from my parents if I didn't make an effort. The sundress was off the shoulders and white with a blue pattern. Greg always said my dark brown hair and olive complexion contrasted nicely with the colors. "Got to do everything I can to support you."

"Greg?" Mom called from the kitchen. "Please come in and join us. We were just sitting down for dinner."

"You had me at dinner," Greg called back before capturing my hand in his.

As we walked into the kitchen, Dad was already laying an additional plate on the table. "We gotta make sure the big baseball legend himself gets fed."

"Especially for tonight's game." Greg marched over to the end cabinet and opened it, grabbing another fork and knife. "I still can't believe it."

"Yeah, time goes by fast." Mom carried over the steaks to the table, placing them right in the center. "If you think it's quick now, just wait until you get our age." She patted Greg's shoulder as she headed back to grab the steamed vegetables.

"No, that's not it." Greg took a deep breath, savoring the aroma. "It's the scout that's coming."

"Scout?" Mom pulled her seat out from the table and sat.

"Your Dad wasn't able to meet me for lunch today so we haven't heard anything." Dad sat and picked up his fork from the table.

Yay, here he goes again. Let's hear all about the hoity-toity scout. I plopped into my seat and grabbed my glass of water.

"Someone from Bloodshed Academy is coming to meet me." Greg couldn't keep the huge grin from his face. "Can you believe it?"

Dad startled, and his fork pinged off the table while Mom's face turned a shade of white.

"Say what now?" Dad straightened in his seat and cleared his throat.

"Right?" Greg grinned as he cut a large piece of his steak and then took a big bite. "It's amazing."

Although Mom and Dad's faces didn't show looks of amazement. They almost looked scared, and I had no clue why.

CHAPTER TWO

To say dinner was tense would be an understatement. Greg talked the entire time about Bloodshed Academy and what it meant for someone from their pack to finally get an invitation. Mom and Dad only nodded their heads and replied in one or two words, which was starkly different than normal.

As Greg and I walked out into the foyer, Mom and Dad followed behind.

"Honey, I'm not feeling so well." Mom placed a hand on her stomach and then shot Greg a sympathetic smile. "I'm sorry, but I don't think I'll be able to make the game tonight."

"You had said something earlier about not feeling well." Dad touched her shoulder and shook his head. "Is it getting worse?"

It's funny because I don't remember her saying anything earlier about not feeling well. In all fairness though, I had been rushing to school since I had overslept.

"Yeah, but I hate missing the baseball game." Mom

sighed and gave me a small smile. "It'd be kinda nice if you stayed home to help take care of me."

Was she being serious? She and Dad had been all about this game up until this very moment. "What?"

"I really need her there with me." Greg threw his arm around my shoulders and tugged me into his chest. "She's my good luck charm."

His musky cologne nearly made me choke. Who the hell wears cologne when they're going to play a game? He's the damn pitcher, so he's one of the sweatiest ones, too. "It's the last baseball game of my senior year." I hated being this way because my parents usually didn't ask me for a lot. But there was something inside me telling me I needed to go.

"Yeah, but you can always hang out with your friends another night." Dad winked at me and pouted. "Please don't make me take care of her all by myself. You know how she gets when she's not feeling well."

In Dad's defense, Mom did get overdramatic and diva-ish when she didn't feel well.

"Sir, I really need her with me." Greg's arm stiffened around me, and a low growl rumbled in his chest.

An alpha wolf doesn't like not being listened to. If Dad wasn't careful, Greg's wolf was going to come out.

Dad glanced at my mother and then sighed. "Fine, but come back home right after the game. The scout is here for Greg, so it'd be best if you didn't interfere."

"Sure, I can have Ian bring her back." Greg dropped his arm from my shoulder and opened the door. "Come on, I can't be late for warm-ups."

Yes, we must rush. The world would come to a halt if Greg wasn't there. Those words were at the tip of my tongue, but I swallowed them down like a bitter pill. I didn't feel like fighting with him tonight.

As I turned to step out the door, Mom grabbed my arm and tugged me toward her so she could look me in the eyes. *Make sure your necklace stays on you, no matter what. Promise me.*

Ever since last week, she'd been nagging me about my necklace. I didn't understand why it was so important to her. *Yes, I promise.*

"Is everything okay?" Greg's brows furrowed, and he glanced at where mom was clutching my arm.

"Yes, fine." Mom released her tight grip and giggled a little too loudly. "I'm just feeling off and hate not being there. I better get to bed." She turned to walk down the hallway.

"Both of you be safe," Dad said as his eyes firmly met mine. "If something feels off, get back here immediately."

Something was definitely going on, and it was freaking me out. "Of course."

Why are your parents being so weird? Greg took my hand and pulled me out the door.

No clue. I mean, it's my senior year, but it's not like I'm leaving the pack or anything. Although he was, and I was so damn jealous. At least, I'd get a little freedom away from him. Sometimes I felt like he was suffocating me and I'd never be able to find air.

"Hey." He stopped at the passenger door and gave me a smile. "You aren't worried about me leaving, are you?"

"No, not really." I gazed down and let my dark hair hide my face. I didn't want him to catch my relieved features.

"This shouldn't change anything between us." He placed his index finger under my chin and lifted my face. "I'll be back during breaks and stuff."

He was going for reassurance, but we both hoped everything would change. "We ... um ... better go. You'll be late."

Slowly, he turned. "Yeah, you're right." He walked around the front of the truck and got in the cab.

I took a deep breath and opened the passenger door. I stepped onto the ledge and slid onto the seat of the F-150. Of course, it was only a year or two old, which didn't help us blend in with the other students very well. "Why don't we just run there?" I cringed because the words slipped out before my filter kicked in.

"You know why." He started the truck and frowned at me. "It's not like we can take our clothes with us in that form. Besides, what if someone saw us stepping out from the woods. The school is going to be packed with people attending the game."

His condescending attitude really rubbed my wolf the wrong way. It growled and bared its teeth inside me. I struggled with the animal and the expected behavior that a submissive wolf exhibited.

Silence descended inside the truck, and my eyes were glued on the houses that we passed by. Our entire pack lived in the subdivision, which made it easy for meetings and running under a full moon.

It didn't take long for us to reach the high school. The sun was setting, and the baseball field lights flashed on. There were several students and parents there already, including Ian, Darren, Sheila, and Greg's dad, Jerry.

"You were making me nervous." Greg's dad laughed as he approached us. "I expected you to be here long before now."

"Sorry, I went to pick up Rave. Her parents insisted I stay and eat." Greg reached into the bed of the truck and grabbed his baseball bag. "But I'm here now and ready to play." His eyes glowed ever so slightly, revealing his wolf's excitement.

"Well, the recruiter should be here any second." His dad glanced around and frowned, checking his watch. "They said they'd be here by now."

"Maybe he got stuck in traffic or something." Greg tucked his red Indian's baseball shirt into his pants. "Come on, I've gotta get warmed up."

"Alright, I'll let you know when the scout gets here." Greg's dad smacked his back as he walked by. "I'm so proud of you, son."

I'm sure he was too. It seemed like fate favored some over others. Greg got to fully embrace his wolf and very likely go to the most prestigious Academy for only the strongest supernaturals. My wolf whimpered, and she took a deep breath. We had to hold it together at least until graduation. I was hoping that the stress from senior year was the reason why my wolf was getting so antsy. In a week's time, it should be all behind me.

"It's about time you got here, man," Ian shouted from shortstop as Greg hit the field.

Greg placed his hat on his head and pulled out his glove. "I'm right on time." He balled his fist and smacked it on the inside of his glove, taking his place on the pitcher's mound. "Let's get going."

Darren saluted Greg from first base. "Whatever you say, boss." Then, he took a step and threw the ball at Greg.

"I hope you're as proud of him as we are." Jerry kept his eyes on his son and took a step closer to me, talking in a near whisper.

I was positive the right answer wasn't that I couldn't care less. "Of course."

"Good." Jerry nodded his head, and his body became a little less tense. "Now don't get me wrong. Susan and I are praying each night that you both choose each other to become mates. But we just want to make sure you aren't going to try to talk him into staying."

It's kind of funny that they thought I had so much influence over Greg. "Don't worry. I won't."

"See, this is why you two make such a good couple." He smiled and bumped his shoulder into mine. "Both of you look out for each other's best interest."

Sure, that's exactly what I'm doing. Granted, I'm happy for him. Although this would give me a chance to figure things out on my own. Greg thought we always had to be going and hanging out with both wolves and humans. It'd be nice to have a break ... to breathe.

"Hey, guys." Sheila strolled up with Susan by her side. Both wore identical red shirts with Indians written on them.

"Are they here yet?" Susan walked over and kissed Jerry on the lips.

"No, not yet." Jerry glanced around and shrugged. "I'm sure they'll be here soon though."

"I can't believe my baby might get accepted into their program." Susan smiled so wide that it had to hurt her face.

Maybe one day, I'd be that happy.

"Wanna grab a seat before they get full?" Sheila nodded toward the bleachers.

"Yeah, sure." I'd hoped to find a seat before she got here. Sheila wasn't so bad, but her blatant need for male attention made me rather uncomfortable.

"Sweet!" She headed toward the bleachers, and as she passed by the fence, she smiled. "Hey, boys."

"Hey!" The second baseman grinned back at her. "Looking good.'

"Aw, thanks." She winked at him and then turned so she was marching up the red bleachers.

"You know you can't date humans." That wasn't a rule a

long time ago, but now it was law. If a human and a wolf reproduced, it either caused a woman to die during birth or resulted in major deformities.

"Yes, I know, Mrs. Rule Follower." Sheila took a seat and rolled her eyes. "It's just harmless flirting. Unlike some here, I don't have an alpha that's crazy about me."

I wasn't sure if he was crazy about me though. "Still, you don't need to lead them on." I sat next to her and was grateful she chose a section right next to the stairs. At least when I got bored, I had an easy escape.

"So, what do you think will happen with you and Greg when he leaves for Bloodshed?" Sheila glanced at her nails and rubbed her fingers over the newly painted, bright red nail polish.

"I don't know." For once, I didn't have to lie. "I guess time will tell."

Sheila pursed her lips to the side. "You're not going to try getting him to stay and lock it in?"

The thought of locking it in made me cringe. "No, it's what's best for him. I'll figure out my own path too."

"Well, you're a lot nicer than me." She shrugged and stared at the ball field. "I'd be begging him to stay."

Yeah, I was nice. That's the reason I was so supportive. "What are you going to do after graduation?"

"I'm not sure yet." Sheila pursed her lips and sighed.

"Well, it's only a week away." I don't know why I was pushing her. "You probably should figure it out."

"You know what?" She narrowed her eyes at me and frowned. "If I wanted to hang out with my Mom, I would've stayed home and not come here. So back off."

"Sorry, I was just trying to help." Maybe I overstepped my boundaries.

"Well, I don't want that kind of help." She crossed her arms and sighed.

Silence descended between us with only the sound of people taking their seats, some low chatter, and the sounds of all the players taking their positions could be heard. The other team was dressed in royal blue with Dodgers written across their chests.

As the away team began their batting line up, Sheila turned toward me. "If my boyfriend was potentially leaving in the near future, I'd be a wreck. So why aren't you?"

Most committed wolves can't stand to be apart for long, and for mates, it's almost impossible. Obviously, I was acting strange ... maybe I could play it off as being submissive. "It's what he wants."

Greg stared the batter down and then stepped forward, pitching the ball. The batter swung but was too late. The ball was already in the catcher's glove.

"Strike one," The ref said, lifting a finger in the air.

"I'm thirsty." I needed to get away for a few moments and get my thoughts together. I stood and began my descent down the stairs.

"Cool. Grab me a coke too?" Sheila called after me.

Needing space, I just nodded and kept my focus on getting away. Something sweet tickled my nose as I reached the ground. It smelt like cotton candy, and my mouth began to water. They only have the bagged kind at the concession stand, so it didn't make sense to smell it so strongly.

As I made my way to the concession stand, I could hear loud cheers as the ump yelled, "You're out."

At least Greg was doing well. There was no line at the concession stand, so I was able to walk right up to the window. "I'd like two cokes and a hotdog." Maybe a little bit of over-processed meat would help calm my nerves.

The girl turned and got my order when someone stepped behind me. The sweet scent filled my nose again and confirmed it wasn't from the concession stand. It was from the person standing right behind me. I forced myself not to turn. It had to be a supernatural because it was a natural scent, not from perfume or cologne.

"Here you go." The girl put the items on the counter, and then her eyes widened at the person behind me. "Oh, hello."

I grabbed a drink and the hot dog when a pale, smooth hand reached for the second cup.

"It looks like you could use some assistance." His voice was alluring and smooth.

However, my wolf growled, and it was hard holding back the sound from my throat. I turned around and became somewhat breathless. "I ..."

"Thank you is usually what most people say when someone does something nice." He smiled, making his blue eyes sparkle even though the sun was setting. He arched his eyebrow, which set off his short blond hair.

"Well, I'd hate for you to go through the trouble." I immediately registered what type of supernatural he was. He was a fucking vampire. "So, I'll be on my way."

"No, no." His smile turned into a smirk, and he took a step closer, infiltrating my space. "I insist. It wouldn't be very gentlemanly if I didn't help a damsel in distress."

"I'm not a damsel in distress." The guy may be sexy as hell, but that was part of a vampire's allure. Most stories and movies weren't accurate about any of the supernaturals, but they nailed it on the vampire. They were meant to be charismatic and charming. The best way to explain the creature was to compare one to a sociopath. They knew right and wrong but usually didn't give a crap. I grabbed the drink from his hand, causing the liquid to spill over the sides.

He smashed his lips together as if he was trying to hide his smile.

It didn't work though.

"Do I amuse you?" Yes, my fingers may have been wet from the Coke, but I refused to admit it.

"That's one way to look at it." He placed his hand over his mouth. Still, his cheeks were raised, so him trying to hide his laughter didn't work. "Let me grab you some napkins."

"No, I think you've done enough." I leaned back on my heels and took off toward the bleachers. For once, I was hurrying to be with Sheila instead of escaping her.

I didn't hear any footsteps behind me, but that was the thing with vampires. They were agile and quick. My heart began to race in my chest, but I refused to alarm the others. Still, why was there a vampire here? I wasn't sure I wanted to know the answer.

CHAPTER THREE

"Are you okay?" Sheila asked as I slid back into my seat behind her.

"Uh ... yeah. Why?" I needed to calm down and get my act together.

"Because you're pale as anything, and it's almost as if you've seen a ghost." She reached over and grabbed one of the drinks. "Eww ... Did you drink out of both of them?"

"No, I spilled some of yours when I was gathering everything." She didn't give me any money, and now she was complaining. It figured.

"Well, Greg has struck out two batters." She glanced around and frowned. "I'm kind of surprised that the scout isn't here. I hope he gets here before the game is over."

"They aren't recruiting him for his baseball skills." It made no sense that everyone was making such a big deal about a recruiter coming for the game.

"He dominates the field." Sheila rolled her eyes and shook her head. "That alone shows how much of a leader he is."

I bit my tongue. I didn't need to argue with her because, at the end of the day, it was irrelevant. The sweet scent once again filled my nose.

"Hey, are you sure you're okay?" For the first time ever, she really looked at me with concern in her eyes.

"Sorry, I'm just a little off." A prickly sensation crawled down my spine, and I tapped into my wolf's hearing. All I heard were the sounds of a ball hitting a bat, the crowd cheering, and some kids playing tag in the open grassy area. Nothing sounded out of sorts, but I couldn't shake the feeling that I was being watched.

Sheila jumped to her feet and started screaming. "Get him at first!"

My eyes went back to the game and watched as Ian threw the ball to Darren. Darren caught the ball as the runner ran on first.

"Safe!" Yelled the umpire.

"Dammit." Sheila slumped back on the seat. She sighed and glanced over at me. "Look, it's just now settling in. I'm sure you guys will make it work."

If only that was what was bothering me. "Yeah, you're right." For some reason, I didn't want to alert the others. My wolf wanted to be the one to call the shots with this guy.

I glanced over my shoulder, and of course, tall, blond and mysterious was right there. He lifted his hand and wiggled his fingers at me.

Who the hell was this guy? I stood and held his gaze. "I've got to run to the bathroom."

"Why didn't you go on the way to the concession stand?" Sheila asked, but her eyes were still locked on the baseball field.

Good, it'd be easier to slip away again. "Sorry, I didn't need to go a few minutes ago." Without any further explanation, I ran down the steps and behind the bleachers that were near the woods.

Yes, I was being stupid, but reinforcements weren't far away. That's how I was justifying it.

"I'm surprised you came out here alone." He appeared on the other side of the bleachers, heading straight toward me. "Don't you realize what I am?"

"A leech, right?" As soon as those words left my mouth, I wished I could take them back.

"Oh, wolves have a sense of humor after all?" His face appeared as if it was made of stone. He wasn't giving anything away.

"Why are you here?" I had to figure out why a vampire would show up now. It made no sense.

He tilted his head and narrowed his eyes. "Didn't they tell you?"

My heart stopped. Is this why my parents were acting so strange? They knew a vampire would be here. "No, they didn't."

"Well, then. For once, I get to make the introduction and share the ever so lovely news." He chuckled at the end and began to move closer to me.

"I won't be your dinner if that's what you're getting at." I didn't back away. I wouldn't act like prey. Even if he took me down, it would be with me fighting 'til the end.

"You know, when I first laid eyes on you earlier, I thought that somehow she was wrong, but now I'm not so sure." Now he was only a few feet away from me, and his candy cotton scent picked up in the breeze.

"What are you talking about?" This one time, I let my wolf take control but didn't allow the shift. A low growl came from my throat, and I lifted my chin defiantly.

"There she is." A smile filled his face, and his body began to relax. "I'm the recruiter from Bloodshed."

Wait. If he was the recruiter, why was he standing here with me? "Oh ... Well, Greg is playing in the baseball game, but I'm sure he'll make time for you after."

"Why would I want to talk to him?" His forehead creased, and he scratched his head.

"I thought you were coming to recruit him." None of this was making any sense.

"No, I'm here for you." His words were clear and direct.

"But a girl can't be an alpha." Those were the words my parents had told me ever since I was a child. "I'm not eligible to be there."

"That's not true at all." He raised both hands in the air. "Hell, the headmaster is a woman and the toughest person I've ever met. She's the one who told me how to find you."

"I don't understand." I didn't want to get my hopes up. Maybe someone was playing a trick on me. "Is this a joke?"

"Okay, let's try this again. A redo if you will." He held his hand out toward me and smiled. "Hi, I'm Cole, a recruiter for Bloodshed Academy."

This had to be a dream or a nightmare. At this point, I wasn't really sure which way this would go. "Hi, I'm Raven."

"Nice to meet you." He extended his right hand and reached for mine. "I promise I won't bite ... unless you want me to."

I wasn't sure if he was laughing or hitting on me. I reluctantly took his hand and shook it. "I thought you were trying to make a good impression."

He chuckled as he crossed his arms in front of him. "No. I think it's you who should be trying to make a good impression."

"If this is some kind of joke Ian is playing on me, tell him to go jump off a cliff." That's the only way this would make any sense.

"Hey, whoa." He approached me slowly as if I was a rabid animal. "I swear. This is no joke. I don't know why you're assuming I'm here for …" He paused and tapped his finger to his lip. "What's his name again?"

"Greg," I growled in my throat and then took a steadying breath. I couldn't let this asshole know just how riled up he was getting me. "You called his father last night to tell him you were coming to meet him."

"Wolves." He chuckled and smirked. "People say vampires hear what they want. Every supernatural is guilty of it just like *Greg's* father."

"Okay, so what did he misunderstand?" Instead of arguing the fact, I decided to turn logic around on him.

"Well, I did call him …"

"See." I interrupted him and cheered in my head.

"You didn't let me finish." Cole lifted a hand and waved it in circles. "May I continue?" His eyes filled with mirth.

"Fine." If he was going to play games, so could I. "You may."

"But I only said I was coming to meet one of his pack members." He dropped his hands, and any trace of mirth vanished. "As I said; you're the one we want."

My heart picked up, and my stomach felt as if it was performing somersaults. "Me … But why?"

"Do you ever feel like you're battling something inside of you?" He moved so there was only an inch of space between us. "That you want to become unhinged?"

That's exactly how I'd been feeling lately. Like if I didn't contain my inner animal, I would explode and raise havoc. "Yes." Something inside me felt freer. Like I was stepping away from my denial and accepting a small portion of what I tried to keep hidden.

"We've all been there, and that's what the academy is really about." The sparkle in his eyes vanished, and he touched my cheek with his fingertips. "You're stronger than any of us realized. For you to keep your wolf contained must be a constant struggle, and not one many people could handle."

Unease filtered through me. I've tried so hard to keep her contained, and it was disconcerting that he could read me that easily. "How will going there help?"

"Your natural instincts are to be on top of the hierarchy." He dropped his hand, but his eyes still held me in place. "Bloodshed will encourage you to rank higher and to finally become one with your supernatural side."

"But I know my wolf." He acted as if I were clueless about myself. "She's a part of me."

"It's hard to explain, but you'll see soon enough when you get there." Cole patted my arm like I was one of his college buddies.

"I didn't say whether I would go or not." I didn't like how he was making my decisions for me.

"If you don't, your wolf will get stronger, and you won't be able to contain her." He closed his eyes and shuddered. "Believe me, I've seen it happen once, and it wasn't pretty."

"Are you trying to scare me?" This random guy ... no wait, vampire, just showed up and invited me to Bloodshed Academy. It was hard to believe. He had to be up to something. Even though I tried to convince myself to be suspicious, my wolf instincts were getting excited.

"I wish that was it." After a brief pause, he took a step back. "Look, I came here and scouted you out. You're legit even if you're out of sync with your wolf. I'll be back after graduation to pick you up." He turned so his back was facing me.

"You don't know my answer, though." What kind of school just assumed you were going to agree?

He stopped in his tracks and glanced over his shoulder. "You've got a lot to learn. When someone gets invited to Bloodshed, there is only one answer."

"I know most people would kill to get in there. Most jump at the opportunity as soon as it permits." This arrogant asshole assumed he knew my answer, which made me ornery as hell. "But I'm leaning toward no."

A smile slowly grew across his face and then turned into a smirk. "It's cute that you think you can truly make the decision."

It was my future to decide even if I chose to stay here and be miserable. "Of course, I do. It is my choice."

His ice-blue eyes somehow seemed colder. "No one can reject Bloodshed Academy. There are dire consequences if you do."

"Are you threatening me?" He's a fucking vampire and on my turf. He had some nerve.

"No, I'm not." His sweet scent seemed to turn a little sour. That happened when vamps got angry. "But no one rejects the academy and survives. You best learn that now." He took a step back and scowled. "I'll see you next week." And just like that, he disappeared.

I stood there breathing heavily with my wolf taking control. I was about to shift, but I couldn't do that here and now.

Loud cheers from the crowd rang in my ears, and everything began to blur. If I didn't get my act together, Cole's words could come true. My wolf instincts were calling me, and it was hard resisting the pull. I fell to the ground and curled into a ball as the war within me fought for dominance.

CHAPTER FOUR

The sun shone into my room, causing me to pull the blankets over my head. Today was the day I graduated, which meant a later start, but dreams had been plaguing me since that night at the baseball field.

It didn't help that Sheila wound up taking me home because Greg was upset that the recruiter never showed. He was arguing with his Dad, thinking he must have blown it for him. If I had added that the recruiter had shown but wanted me, things would've escalated more than it already had.

You'd think I'd have been excited to put high school behind me, but right now, time seemed to be moving too fast. I just needed to get through the day in one piece.

I got up, dressed, and put some makeup on, but my mind seemed to be elsewhere. I was only going through the motions.

A knock on the door startled me. Damn it, a wolf should never be taken by surprise. I was so preoccupied with my thoughts, ignoring the world. A light vanilla scent floated into the room. "Come in."

"Hey, honey." Mom opened the door and entered the room. Her dark brown hair was pulled back into a ponytail, and her forehead was lined with worry. "Are you okay?"

"Yeah, why?" It probably didn't help that I had been jumpy the past few days. Almost as if I thought Cole was going to appear out of thin air.

"Ever since you came home from the baseball game, you've been acting strange." She pursed her lips and tapped her fingers on her black slacks. "Even Greg has said something. I just want to make sure you're okay. Did anything happen?"

I'm surprised that Greg noticed how I'd been acting. He'd been so obsessed and angry about the scout never showing. I didn't want to lie to Mom, but at the same time, I felt like the truth should stay hidden. "It's a little surreal. I mean my whole life changes today."

A tight smile flitted across her face. "Yes, it does. Have you figured out what your next steps are? You haven't talked about it for a little while."

Well, that's because apparently, I'm going to a school that no one can refuse. How the hell did that work when I never applied? Although, how peculiar my parents got when the academy was mentioned made me pause. They seemed stressed, and I didn't want to add to their worry until I had to. "I'm thinking fate always has a way of finding you."

Mom's body stiffened and her fingers stilled. "Some things are better kept hidden."

"What do you mean?" They were definitely hiding something from me, and I didn't like it.

Mom took a deep breath and relaxed her shoulders. "I'm sorry honey." She stepped in closer and grabbed my hand. "I'm just having a hard time with you growing up."

With her free hand, she reached and tapped the quarter-moon crescent of my necklace. "The necklace looks perfect on you."

I gave a small smile and paused, making the words I nearly slipped out sit hard in my stomach. I wanted to reassure her, but I didn't want to outright lie to her. If Cole was serious, then he could show at any moment and take me away to the school. For some reason, I didn't think he was kidding either. "It's strange." That was the best I could muster due to the situation.

"Raven, it's time to go." Dad's voice called from the foyer. "We're going to be late."

"Oh, no." Mom dropped her hands back to her sides and sniffed. As she wiped underneath her eye, she chuckled. "Now, look what I've done. Upset us, and if we don't hurry, we'll be late."

At that point, I wasn't sure what to say or do. It felt as though we both were keeping secrets from one another. So I said the only words that were completely safe and true to say. "I love you."

"Baby girl, I love you too." She wrapped her arms around me, giving me one last quick hug before tugging me out the door. "I will say that's the ugliest outfit I've ever seen you in."

To say otherwise would have been a straight out lie. I hated the long red, graduation gowns and hats they made us wear. "Don't get me started."

As we made our way down the stairs, Dad smiled. "Look at our daughter all grown up."

"Hey now, don't start on her." Mom reached over and lovingly squeezed my arm. "I've already cried once. We need to go."

"Fine." Dad walked over and hugged me once. "Let's get going."

Parking was horrendous at the school. The graduation was scheduled to begin in ten minutes, so I was later than what the teachers had required. The parking lot was full, which meant a lot of family and friends were attending the ceremony.

Dad made his own parking spot at the end of the lot, wedging himself between two cars.

I was going to complain, but that wouldn't have done any good.

As I slid out from the backseat, my eyes landed on a shiny, red Audi that had the words Bloodshed Academy written in gothic letters on it. I reread the sticker over and over again, hoping I was only seeing things. Still, with each blink, the words didn't change no matter how hard I wished.

"Rave, are you okay?" Dad moved beside me and followed my gaze. His face paled, and he took a step back. "Liz ..."

"What are you two gaping at?" Mom turned her head and took a sharp intake of breath.

What was I going to do? Maybe it was someone other than Cole that was coming to meet Greg. I mean, he is the strongest alpha next to his father in our pack. Maybe it was all a mix-up or a cruel joke. That definitely had to be it.

"I guess they're here to meet Greg." Mom took a deep breath and shook her head. "We better get going before they don't have any seats left."

"Are you ..." Dad cringed.

"Yes ... Yes, I am." Mom cut him off, and her stance was

rigid once more. "Now let's go. Raven can't miss her only graduation."

The rest of the way into the gym was in awkward silence. Each step of the way, I kept saying over and over in my head that they were here for Greg, not me. That was the only thing that made sense. By the time I reached the double doors that entered the gym, I'd lied to myself that they couldn't be here for me. That was until I took my first step into the gym.

He was right there, leaning against the wall only a few feet away.

A smirk spread across his devilishly handsome face as he raised his hand in the air and wiggled his fingers at me.

That's what he did to me the other night at the baseball game. The image had been burned into my mind.

His blond hair was styled in spikes in the front, and his black shirt hugged his athletic frame. He was hot and knew it, just like every vampire did.

A large, muscular guy beside him turned and faced me. His chocolate eyes seemed to burn into me, and he took a step toward me before stopping. He clenched his hands, and his shaggy brown hair fell into his face a little.

Damn, Cole brought a wolf shifter here. Why would he do that?

"You better hurry and take your seat." Mom glanced over at the two guys that had captured my attention. "Let's go sit on the other side, honey."

"Sounds perfect." Dad placed his hand at the base of my back and guided me to the center of the gym. "Knock 'em dead, honey." He leaned down and kissed the top of my head.

"You do realize I'm only walking across the stage?" I tried to make a light joke, but I couldn't shake the feeling that both of the Bloodshed recruiters were staring straight at me.

Dad ignored my comment, and both he and Mom headed in the opposite direction, looking for a place to sit.

"What's wrong, Raven?" Greg appeared in front of me and smiled brightly.

"Nothing." I couldn't help but steal a glance over my shoulder. Of course, both Cole and his friend were still standing there.

"Oh, okay. Good." He reached up and placed his thumb under my chin, turning my head back in his direction. "Guess what Dad and I saw when we were walking in?"

A growl wanted to emanate from my chest, but I held it in. I hated when Greg treated me like a doll instead of a person. However, there was a growl from behind me.

The muscular boy who was with Cole appeared at my side, staring down Greg. "You should respect her more than that."

"Whoa." Greg lifted his chin and showed his teeth. "Why don't you mind your own business?" *Who the hell is this guy, Raven?*

I've never met him before. To be fair, I had no clue why this guy was acting this way.

"Hey, now." Cole appeared in between the guy and Greg. "It's getting late. Why don't you two go find your place?"

"Oh, you're the recruiter?" Greg tilted his head and crossed his arms over his chest.

"I don't know what you're talking about." Cole pushed his friend in the shoulder, making him back away.

"Well, then we have a problem." Greg's blue eyes began to glow. "Since we hadn't approved any of your kind to come here."

"Thanks, man." Cole glared at his friend for a second before spinning back around to face us. "Yes, I am. But right now, you both need to go and find your seats." He pointed behind where the teachers were climbing the stairs onto the raised platform. "We'll talk afterward."

Any trace of anger was removed from Greg's face. "Of course." He turned around and headed to the seats with a little bit of a skip to his step.

Not wanting to attract any additional attention, I headed straight to my seat, which happened to be right next to Sheila. Right as my bottom hit the seat, she turned my way. "Greg just told us that the vampire from Bloodshed is here now. I can't wait to see what happens after graduation."

Our principal stood at the podium and gave a large smile. "We're glad to have so many people here today to witness their loved ones graduating high school."

Do you think they'll take him right after graduation? Sheila moved in her seat and flipped her hair back. *I thought we'd have him all summer, but if they're here now ... well, maybe they'll take him right after this.*

I have no clue. My stomach was already in knots knowing they weren't here for him, but I didn't want the shit to hit the fan. I'd gladly trade places with her. My wolf side cringed at that thought.

For the rest of the ceremony, I couldn't pay attention to anything. It was an hour later, and the whole time, I focused on what may happen when this was all over. Granted, I'd always known I wasn't going to be able to do everything I wanted because as a pack, we needed to stay together. Still, I'd have some kind of say in my life whether it be that I became a nurse, teacher, or even an accountant. Now it seemed as if any control that I may have had was gone.

Raven, aren't you coming? Sheila patted me on the arm and took off after the front of the line.

I jumped out of my seat and followed behind her. *Thanks.*

What's wrong with you? Sheila glanced over her shoulder and frowned. *You're not acting normal.*

Yeah, I bet she'd like to know. *Nothing, it just feels surreal.*

It wasn't long before it was my turn to go up the stairs. I climbed halfway and waited as they announced Sheila.

"Sheila Wilburn." The principal called out and clapped her hands as Sheila walked across the stage and grabbed her diploma.

"Raven Wright." I can do this. I hit the platform and headed straight to the principal. Mom and Dad cheered while Greg clapped down below.

There were only two other people after me, and the graduation would be over. Now, it was time to face my future.

CHAPTER FIVE

"Oh, honey. We're so proud." Mom was by my side in a flash.

My heart was pounding too hard. I needed to calm down, or everyone would know I was apprehensive.

"Baby, can you believe it." Greg appeared behind me, wrapping his arms around my waist. "We're free from this hell hole."

"It's bittersweet." Jerry shook his head and tilted his head toward mom. "Our babies are grown up, but at least, yours will be staying close."

"That's very true." Dad reached over and slapped Jerry on the back. "But you'll have a fighter when it's all said and done."

"He's already an amazing fighter." Ian appeared beside me but didn't even acknowledge my presence. "I can't wait until he teaches me everything he learns from that school."

"Unfortunately, he's not going to have that opportunity." Cole sauntered over with his buddy right behind him.

"If that's the case, why are you here?" Jerry turned around, and his nostrils flared.

"Because we're here for someone else." The muscular guy stepped forward and towered over Jerry. His mere presence was commanding.

"Oh, really?" Ian's eyes lit up. "Is it me?"

"Come on, Raven." Dad's voice tensed, and he grabbed my hand, pulling me apart from Greg. "It's time to go."

"Actually, that's not possible." Cole appeared in front of my Dad, blocking his path. He looked at me and winked. "See, I told you I'd see you again."

"You've met him before?" Greg's mouth dropped, and his face turned a red shade.

This was the moment I'd been dreading and praying it wouldn't happen. "At your game."

"But you've listened to me for the past week complaining about him never showing up." His breathing increased, and he looked past me to Cole.

"I bet she convinced him of picking her over you." Ian glared at me, and his nose wrinkled.

"You think I'd be so easily persuaded by a pretty face?" Cole's demeanor became rigid, and his face was a stone of indifference.

"What? No." Ian shook his head no and raised both hands. "I just meant ..."

"Well, she's not going with you." Mom stepped in front of me, shielding me from the vampire. She lifted her chin in challenge.

"I agree with Ms. Wright." Greg spread his shoulders and glared. "If I can't go, no one can. I'm the next alpha. Tell them, Dad."

The muscular guy faced Mom down. "If we leave without her, there will be severe repercussions."

"Of course, she'll go with you." Jerry clapped his son on the back.

"Are you being serious?" Greg's mouth dropped, and he jerked back as if he had been slapped. "Dad, you can't be agreeing to this."

"Greg, remember your place." Jerry's eyes glowed as he commanded his son to be silent. "If Bloodshed wants Raven, then so be it."

"What? No." Mom turned to face him with her mouth gaping open.

"Liz, she has to go." Dad's voice was strong, but I heard the rare tremble in it.

This whole situation was strange. I knew it wouldn't be great, but I didn't expect this. My wolf side was brimming with excitement.

"So, there we have it." Cole grabbed my hand and tugged.

His hand was warm and smooth. I'd expected it to be cold, but hell, what did I know. The last time he touched me, I had coke spilled over my hands. I'd only ever been around others like me.

"Hey, is everything okay over here?" The principal walked over and glanced at each one of us.

"I'm sorry. We must've been making a scene." Cole stepped in front of me and placed a hand on his chest. "It's just we're so super excited that our girl has finally graduated. We were just on our way out anyway."

Our girl? Why did that have a nice ring to it?

Why didn't you tell us about this? Mom's words were curt.

I'm sorry. I really didn't think this would happen. The wolf half of me had been excited and anticipating while my human side had been in complete denial.

"Yes, please do." The principal pulled at the neckline of his button-down shirt. "You're making others that are trying to leave out this door feel uncomfortable. They are walking around the whole gym, exiting the other side."

"Let's go outside." Jerry motioned to the door, and Greg grumbled, following along behind him.

As we stepped outside, the parking lot was at a gridlock. Everyone was leaving at the same time, probably meeting family for lunch to celebrate further. Our group marched outside and disappeared into the small wooded area by the school.

I can't believe you didn't tell me. Greg's grasp was firm and rigid. *You knew I wanted to go there.*

It's not my fault. His attitude was pissing me off. It wasn't like I asked to be the one going there instead of him.

"Now, let's get to the point." Jerry turned around to face Cole and his friend. "She can go on one condition."

"Is that so?" Cole chuckled and leaned back a little while crossing his arms.

"Yes." Jerry pointed at his son. "She can go if you take him as well."

"Did you hear that, Rage?" Cole turned and looked at his friend. "It's a buy one, get one free deal."

Rage's eyes were glued on my and Greg's interlocked hands. "The free one isn't appealing at all."

"That's kinda funny." Cole grinned and tapped his fingers on his lip. "You see, he and I never agree, but I guess today changes that."

"What's wrong with my son?" Jerry grew rigid, and his face turned the color of a tomato.

"He's mostly bark and no bite." Rage's voice was raspy and dead sexy.

"And what, she isn't?" Greg dropped my hand and took a step toward them.

I wanted this to all be over, but who knew what was going to happen next.

"It doesn't matter. We were told to come get her," Cole said as he pointed at me. "So that's what we're going to do."

Mom and Dad walked over and gave me a group hug. Dad's comforting voice filled my head. *If you need us, we're only a phone call away.*

I hadn't even thought of that. I wouldn't be able to mind link with them from that far away. *I love you.*

Listen to me. Mom's voice turned urgent. *Don't trust anyone. Make them earn it.* There was an edge to her tone that I'd never heard before.

Dragging this out wasn't going to prevent the inevitable. I took a deep breath and pulled back. *I'll be careful.*

"Well, uh …" Greg refused to look at me and focused on the ground. "See ya later." He turned and stalked off, not even bothering to give me a hug goodbye.

You should be ashamed. Ian shook his head and took a few steps back. *I knew you were opportunistic.*

The last thing I wanted to do was deal with Ian, so I ignored him. He soon huffed and turned around to follow Greg.

"I'm sorry about my son." Jerry's lips spread into a tight smile. "It's just he had his hopes set on it."

"Yeah, but it's not like I asked for this." Even though the thought was becoming more and more appealing, I never dreamed this would happen.

"We need to get going." Cole glanced at his watch and sighed. "If we aren't back to the Academy by ten, it'll get chaotic."

If this wasn't what he considered chaotic, I was afraid to see his definition. I glanced at my parents one last time before turning to follow Rage and Cole.

As we approached the Audi, Rage stepped over and opened the front passenger door.

Now the question was which guy did I want to sit behind? I paused for a moment.

Rage motioned to the door. "I'm not holding this open for my health."

That was not something I had expected. "Oh, I thought you were sitting there."

"The correct response is to sit and tell him 'thank you.'" Cole arched an eyebrow with a smug smile on his face.

My heart hammered against my chest as I headed to the open door and slid past him to sit. Rage was intense, strong, and freaking hot. "Thank you." I took a deep breath, and his earthy scent filled my nose. He smelled like home.

He shut the door, cutting me off from my strange emotion. As he slid behind me, the sense of comfort came back. "Okay, I need to go grab my clothes." I had refused to pack, assuming Cole was messing with me.

"No, you won't need them." Cole started the car and glanced back at his friend. "Can you at least hunker down so I can see backing up?"

"Use the fucking back up camera, moron." Rage crossed his arms and straightened his back so he could sit even higher.

"Backup cameras are for losers who can't drive." Cole leaned over the center console, trying to glance out the back window.

"Well, at least you know why I suggested it to you." Rage quirked an eyebrow and looked down his nose.

A giggle escaped before I could hold it back.

"You are one lucky wolf." Cole reversed quickly. He quickly placed an arm in front of me, holding me against the seat, and slammed on the brakes.

Two large hands gripped my seat. "Did you really think that would work? We have fast reflexes just like your kind."

"It was only a warning." Cole chuckled then opened his mouth. Two long incisors protruded, and the ends looked wickedly sharp.

Any sense of comfort I'd had vanished just like that. It had never fully registered that he was a vampire, at least not until now.

"If you know what's in your best interest, fear isn't something you want others to smell." Cole licked his lips and stared right at my neck. "It makes the predator in a vampire come out."

Yeah, like that was going to make me feel better. I counted to ten and let my wolf surface a little more. I always felt stronger in that form.

"There you go." Cole focused back on the road, and soon we were pulling out of the parking lot.

"Where exactly are we going?" Probably a stupid question, but I wanted to know.

"You haven't even researched to find out the university's location?" Rage's voice was filled with disbelief.

"Honestly, no." I glanced out the window, watching as my city passed by. "I never even considered Bloodshed an option."

"This has to be a mistake." Rage groaned from the backseat. "Tell me this is a joke and we aren't taking her there."

What happened to Mr. Nice guy? I shouldn't have been surprised. Normally in my experience, muscular hot guys were always douches.

"No, it's not." Cole tapped his fingers along the wheel and glanced back at Rage. "I saw a glimmer of it, but nothing more than that."

"You do realize I'm right here." I despised when people

did this sort of shit. Greg and Ian did this to me all the freaking time.

"Have you done any research about the school?" Rage leaned forward, and his dark short hair was now in complete disarray.

No, I hadn't at all, but I'd be damned if I were to admit it to him. "Yeah, it's where all the alphas go." One point for me.

"Gods, is that all you know?" Rage leaned back and threw his hands in the air. "She's going to get herself killed. Let's take her back right now."

"Stop it." Cole rolled his eyes and shook his head. "You're being a drama queen."

"Are you fucking kidding me?" Rage huffed and crossed his arms. "Who found her?"

I clenched my hands together, trying to prevent myself from punching the guy. He had some nerve.

"What is wrong with you?" Cole's forehead wrinkled as he messed with the air conditioning knob. "Here, let's cool you off. It was Isadora who found her."

"Shit. Okay." Rage dropped his arms to his sides and sighed. "Then we need to school her before we get there."

"Oh, how you've changed into such a caring recruiter all of a sudden." Cole chuckled and glanced over his shoulder. "But yea, let's help her out. I'd hate for her to get eaten on the first day."

"Eaten?" Seriously. Please tell me he's kidding.

"Pretty much, especially if you can't handle yourself." Rage pulled out his phone and began typing.

"This school is so much more than what you think." Cole pulled onto the interstate, heading South toward Chattanooga. "It's about who is the strongest and smartest."

"Yeah, like I said, alpha." The description for the school was what an alpha was supposed to encompass.

"No, you can have a stupid leader." Cole glanced at Rage. "I mean, look at him."

"Bloodshed is a university like no other." Rage leaned forward, turning his back to Cole and his face to me. "There isn't a set date for your graduation. It's a series of trials and tribulations. You either graduate or fail."

"And in some cases, die." Cole leaned over so he could see me and winked. "Let's hope it's not the latter for you."

"What do you mean by trials?" No one had ever mentioned this before. I was beginning to think I shouldn't have come.

"That, my dear, is something we aren't allowed to tell you." Cole reached over and shoved Rage back in his seat.

"Dude, not cool." Rage grumbled and crossed his arms. "We can't tell you what you'll go through. Each student has their individual needs, and no one student is the same."

"Think about it. Do you think vampires have the same strengths and weaknesses as any other shifter?" Cole placed his hands on the steering wheel and focused. "Now then, take it a step further. Do you think Rage has the same temperament, strength, and personality as you?"

When he put it that way, it made sense. I guessed there wasn't a cookie-cutter way to each person's development. "Still, we would have a few things in common."

"Right." Cole glanced at me and grinned. "But not everything."

The farther away I got from home, the more uncertain I became. I wasn't sure what to expect anymore.

CHAPTER SIX

The entire ride to Bloodshed went by both painfully slow and too fast for me. We continued to travel in silence except for when Rage grumbled that he was hungry and we had to run through a McDonald's drive-thru for his sustenance. He had wanted me to eat some of the food too, but I couldn't. My stomach revolted at the mere idea of food.

When we cruised through New Orleans, I wasn't surprised. Even if I hadn't looked into this university, it would make sense that it would be in a paranormal hot spot. What I wasn't prepared for though was Cole pulling into Tulane University.

Even though it was dark, with my wolf's eyesight, I could see clearly. It contained well maintained older buildings, a lot of trees, and an outside feeling all around. Was this some kind of joke? "I thought we were going to Bloodshed Academy."

"You do realize there are humans that live here too, right?" Rage quirked an eyebrow at me, and humor-filled his eyes.

"Yeah, but ..." I still wasn't following what that had to do with supernaturals.

"Rage, she's onto something." Cole's blue eyes lit, and a predatory grin crossed his face. "Why stay hidden when we could creep everyone out? Maybe we could put a statue of me out here and have blood dripping down my face."

"Instead of acting like an asshole, you could just explain it to her." Rage leaned over and punched Cole in the arm.

Despite Cole being smaller than Rage, he didn't budge an inch. "Aw, did I hurt yours or her feelings? Right now, I'm having a hard time telling the difference."

"I kind of agree with him." I pointed to Rage and crossed my hands over my chest.

"Of course, you would." Cole stuck his tongue out at me. "Shifters before misters."

"That doesn't even make sense." Rage's forehead creased, and he shook his head.

"You both are shifters and," Cole said as he pointed between him and Rage, "we're boys, so misters."

"Oh, dear God." Rage rubbed the bridge of his nose. "When was the last time you fed?"

"Not too long ago, but I wouldn't mind feeding off someone here." His blue eyes landed on me.

"Don't even think about it." A low growl vibrated deep in Rage's chest.

"Can we get back to the university?" Cole was too high energy. I thought vampires were supposed to be all moody and depressed.

"Bloodshed is hidden by this school." Rage leaned forward in his seat again, focusing solely on me.

Having his undivided attention was unnerving. It sort of felt like there were butterflies in my belly. "Where?"

"The school is known for its exclusivity, which means

most of the applicants are supernaturals. Tulane is the name that humans know it as, and even a few of them attend. But the back section is spelled to repel humans, and that's where Bloodshed is hidden." Rage pointed out the window.

We came upon a gray stoned building that had an imposing fence. A gold emblem with Bloodshed Academy was attached to the gates.

"I thought you said this place was a secret from humans." There was a huge ass sign that stated it all right there.

Cole stopped in front of the gates and pulled out his phone. He pressed a button, and the doors began to swing open. "They wouldn't have ever made it this far."

Within moments, we were driving through the gate and took a left toward a full parking lot. The gray stone building was huge, and there were two smaller buildings behind it.

The main thing that comforted me was all the trees surrounding the whole campus. At least there was ample space for me to run.

"Welcome to your new home." Cole pulled into a reserved spot and lifted both hands up.

Yeah, I wasn't sure it was quite home yet.

Rage swung open his door and gracefully exited.

That's really nice. He didn't even say goodbye. So, when my door opened for me, I was surprised to see Rage standing there.

"Oh ... uh ... thanks." Yeah, real smooth, Raven. I clambered out, trying not to feel awkward.

Cole leaned on the hood of the car and used his arms to prop his head up. "I could watch this all day."

I glared at him and leaned on my back leg. "Watch what?"

"Oh, no." He stood and waved both hands in front of himself. "Please, ignore me, and both of you continue this tragic excuse for flirting."

"Cole, shut the fuck up." Rage gave him a warning look.

"Aw." Cole grinned while wiggling his eyebrows. "Did I hit a nerve?"

Between Rage's earthy smell filling my nose and the testosterone match these two were in, I had to get away. I took several steps in the direction of the school when the sound of crashing footsteps in the woods to our left caught my attention. It didn't sound like a wolf. The feet landed too hard and so loud it had to be a much larger shifter like a bear or dragon.

My wolf surged forward, asking for control, but I shouldn't be worried. Surely Cole and Rage would alert me if something was off.

However, the creature was getting closer and closer.

My heart began to race, and I glanced back to see Cole and Rage still bickering.

A loud roar filled my ears as one of the largest bears I'd ever seen came barreling out of the trees straight toward me.

My wolf forced its way to the front, and then blackness engulfed me.

THE SCENT of lavender filled my nose, and the tapping of someone's foot woke me. *Where the hell am I?* My eyelids were so heavy. I slowly opened them. There were rails on both sides of my bed, and the white ceiling seemed higher than normal.

"Sleeping beauty has finally awakened." Cole's polished voice seemed to dance across the room.

"Now isn't the time for humor." The lady who sat by the door stood and made her way to me. Each time she took a step, her black heels clicked, and she adjusted her red suit jacket over her matching skirt. "You both better be glad that I showed up when I did."

Cole's smile left his face, and he glanced at the ground. "You're right."

Rage remained silent, but his dark eyes were on me.

"What happened?" Flashes of the bear racing toward me flitted through my mind. "Oh, God. Did I hurt him?"

The room filled with silence.

"Right now, what we need to focus on is that you don't have control over your wolf." The lady's sharp features were emphasized by the short, dark hair that barely reached past her ears. Her sparkling green eyes were a stark contrast to everything else. "My recruiters weren't very observant, which is disappointing, but in their defense, we hadn't expected you to be that out of sync with your wolf."

"But my wolf and I are fine." I was lying, and somehow this woman knew it.

Cole frowned. "I told you there seemed to be some kind of disconnect. I saw it the first time I saw her."

"Even more reason you should've been paying attention." Her stern voice echoed in the room. "You even had Rage go with you in case you needed help."

Of course, that's why Rage was there. Great, now he thinks I'm weak and stupid. "I don't know what happened, but I've never blacked out before."

"That's because you'd never felt that threatened before." The lady sighed and walked over to me. "This is not how I expected our first meeting to happen. Nonetheless, this is it. As your headmaster, the first thing we need to work on is your connection with your wolf. You won't even last a full year if you don't connect with your wolf completely."

Those words didn't sit well with me. "Are you threatening me?"

Her eyes turned hard, and she frowned. "Take it how you will." She glanced at both of the guys. "I expect better, or there will be consequences." She turned with her head high and walked out the door.

"Is she always like that?" A headmaster should be supportive and caring. That woman was not like that at all.

"Yeah, Isadora is always like that, but we messed up." Rage closed his eyes and shook his head. "How are you?"

Is he being serious? "Well, let's see. I was forced to go with you guys to come here, a bear charged me, and I blacked out. Oh ... and the headmaster just threatened me. I'd say it's been a pretty shitty day."

"See," Cole said, grinning at Rage and pointing at me, "we're totally going to be best friends."

A low growl emanated from Rage's chest. "I sure hope not."

"You better stop." Cole arched an eyebrow, and the humor fell from his face. "She's going to need a friend and someone on her side."

"And it can't be me?" Rage's voice turned low and raspy. If I hadn't been so upset, I'd probably be a drooling mess at this very moment.

"You know why." Cole's face was a mask of indifference.

"Guys, I'm really tired." I couldn't handle this, not now. I needed a bed and none of their bickering.

One of the guys' phones rang, but neither moved to answer it.

"That's the fourth time it's rung in the last ten minutes."

Cole crossed his arms and tilted his head down. "Aren't you going to answer it?"

Rage took a deep breath and stared straight into Cole's eyes. "No."

"The longer it takes you, the worse it's going to be." Cole marched toward me and smiled. "Come on, let's get you to your room."

"I have a room?" Something weird was going on between them, and I didn't have the energy to even want to figure it out.

"Of course you do." Cole glanced at Rage. "You need to go deal with that situation before things get any worse."

"Fine." Rage's dark eyes glanced once more at me. "Sleep well."

"You're lucky." Cole gently grabbed my arm, pulling me from the room. "You only have one roommate, which is rare."

For some reason, I hadn't even contemplated that I'd have a roommate. "Oh, is she nice?"

"She's been at the university for a year now, so she'll be able to help you learn the ins and outs." Cole's warm smile returned to his face.

"Oh, so you guys won't be around any longer?" Why did that bother me? I'd assumed that we would hang out still. Obviously proving how much of a freshman I really was. Wait … What would I be? They didn't have freshmen here. Maybe fresh meat?

"I've already decided we're going to be friends, so there is no getting rid of me." He pulled me down a long hallway. The ceilings were high, and the walls were dark brown.

I glanced behind us, looking for Rage, but almost slipped on the smooth pale floor.

"Hey now, I thought shifters had good balance." Cole slipped his arm around my waist.

"Yeah, I normally do, but I feel off tonight, and I ..." I cut myself off. He didn't have to know I was looking for Rage.

A loud voice echoed from behind us. "Ragey, where the hell have you been?"

Several feet away stood a girl with dark red hair and a figure to die for. She placed her hands on her hips as she glanced down the hallway in front of her.

"Ashley, I told you I had to go with Cole to recruit someone." Rage sighed, and his voice sounded tired.

"Come on, let's go." Cole tugged on me, but for some reason, I had to stay. I couldn't remove my eyes from this Ashley.

"He's never asked you to go on a recruit with him before, so why now?" She pouted, emphasizing her already plump lips. "I've missed you."

"He needed a wolf shifter for back up." Rage appeared but didn't seem to notice both Cole and me standing there.

She eliminated the distance between her and Rage and wrapped her arms around his waist. "Well, you're back now, and that's all that matters." She raised up on her tiptoes and placed her lips upon his.

Not able to watch their kiss, I turned and began moving once more with Cole. Surprisingly, he kept his mouth shut until we made our way through one of the back doors.

The fresh air filled my lungs, and I focused on breathing. I was upset over Rage and that girl even though I had no right to be. So what if his lips were on another girl. I had a boyfriend at home, waiting for me. Somehow reminding myself of that made it worse and not better.

CHAPTER SEVEN

After a few moments, Cole asked, "Hey, are you okay?" He led me toward the building on the left.

Tonight, the humidity was high, and it wasn't even officially summer yet. The moon was full, which tugged on my wolf inside. There was no way I was going to attempt shifting after what happened earlier. "Yeah, just taking it all in." I didn't want Cole to know how upset I was over Rage and his girlfriend.

His eyes narrowed as he examined me but then sighed. "It's a lot. That back there ..."

Oh, hell no. We weren't going to talk about Rage, so I cut him off. "What's my roommate like?"

A small smile spread across his face. "Well, she's no me."

"At least that one prayer was answered." Each step I took made me more nervous than the last. The headmaster already wasn't impressed with me, and now I had to meet some kind of supernatural that would be my roommate. I wasn't even sure what to expect at this point.

"Lookie there." Cole reached over and tapped me on

the nose. "Even when you've had one hell of a day, you still have some bite. Be glad. You'll need it."

"If you were going for comfort, let me tell ya; you failed." If these were his pep talks, I'd have hated to see what the opposite would be.

We reached the building, which was much more modern than the main one. It appeared to be a steel type building with large portions of glass. Many had curtains that were closed so no one could see inside.

"Wait." I needed a minute to collect myself. In one day, my whole world had been ripped apart, and I was off-balance. I needed a chance to center myself before another new obstacle was presented to me.

"Of course." Cole paused and took a step back, giving me space.

Despite what he tries to put off, Cole seemed like a good person. Maybe we'd be friends after all. I didn't have many true friends back home. I always had to be cautious and tried to blend in. Still, look how far that had gotten me. It'd be nice to have a friend that I didn't have to hide from.

I lifted my head and glanced at the moon. It was a crystal-clear night, and the view was gorgeous. A distant howl filled the air. Maybe one day that'll be me.

"It's okay to feel overwhelmed." Cole leaned against the side of the building and smiled. "Each one of us here feels that way pretty regularly."

"Really?" For some reason, that made me calmer. It was nice knowing I wasn't alone.

"Yeah, but the first thing you've got to learn is not to show it." Cole stepped toward me and placed his hands on my shoulders. He leaned in so we were looking eye to eye. "This place is where the cream of the crop is. If you show any weakness, they will pounce. Feel it, talk to me about it, but keep it locked inside if you want to survive."

He was right. The one thing all strong supernaturals wanted to do was dominate others when threatened. I was a new threat coming in and apparently not in sync with my wolf. I was already off to a great start too. "But my wolf and I …"

"It's okay." His normally ice-blue eyes seemed warm. "We are all here because we've got weaknesses. We still aren't ready to be the leader each of us needs to be. You just don't admit it and refuse to break down in front of anyone. Bloodshed is named that for a reason. This is a cutthroat school. You have to keep your friends close and your enemies even closer. Do you understand?"

"So I shouldn't even trust you?" At least back home, we were all one pack.

"I'll let you make that call yourself." Cole dropped his hands to his sides and winked. "Now, let's go get you settled."

Hanging out here wasn't going to fix anything. "Alright, let's do this." I took a deep breath and opened the door.

"Look at you go." Cole chuckled behind me.

I marched through the hallway, which strangely resembled a hotel. The walls were a light grey, and the carpet was a slightly shaggy medium grey. I had no clue where I was heading so I kept going straight and turned down a hallway on the right, which led me into a large lounge area. There was a group of girls sitting on two couches that faced each other.

A coppery smell hit me hard, making me notice the two girls on one couch, drinking from blood bags. The two on the other couch leaned back, talking as if this was an everyday occurrence.

"Are we just going to walk around a while, or are you ready for me to take you to your room?" Cole was attempting to hide a smile, but it didn't work.

"You said to take charge." Did he already forget the conversation we had just a few minutes ago? "So I did."

He raised both hands in the air and chuckled. "True, but it's okay for you to follow and let someone else lead the way when you have no clue where you're going."

Clearly, I was in over my head. "Well, this is going great."

"Come on, Ravey." Cole wrapped his hand around my waist and tugged me to the left where there was a set of elevators.

"Cole?" One of the girls stood and tossed the bag of blood on the couch. Her long, jet-black hair bounced as she made it over to us. She pulled her v-neck hunter green shirt down which made her cleavage more pronounced. "What are you doing here?"

Wow, she hadn't even looked in my direction, acting as if I were invisible.

"Showing our new addition to her room." Cole's hand tightened on my side, and he frowned. "Not that it's any of your business." His voice took on an edge.

"Don't be so mean to Jordan." The other vampire glared at me as she approached. Her fingernails were painted blood red, which almost blended in with the bag she was clutching. Her long, dirty blonde hair fell past her butt, and her light green eyes had a ring of red.

"Madison, why don't you mind your own fucking business?" Cole's cold tone surprised me.

"I've never seen you get so cozy with a new recruit." Jordan's eyes landed on me. The same red ring was around her golden eyes. "Honestly, I haven't seen you this close to any girl that you weren't about to fuck. Should I warn her about you?"

That was surprising seeing as Cole had been nice to me from the start. "Have you ever considered that you were a little too late with that warning?" The words fell from my mouth before I had time to think it through.

Cole's fingers dug into my side, pulling me even closer somehow.

"Who the hell do you think you are?" Jordan's beautiful face contorted into a scowl. "Did I give you permission to talk to me?"

"Well, it's a good thing I didn't ask." My wolf surged forward, and my eyesight began to darken.

"You better restrain your mutt." Jordan spat the words as she wrinkled her nose. "She's beginning to smell like the dog she really is."

"That's enough, you two." Cole took a step into the girls' space, but his normally beautiful face contorted into something completely different. His ice-blue eyes narrowed, and a look of pure disgust filled his face. "Go back to your gossip, and get the hell out of our way."

I was so glad I wasn't on the receiving end because I'd be scared shitless.

"Fine." Madison lifted her chin and grabbed her friend's arm. "Let's leave them to whatever they're doing. It's not like he'll pay any attention to her in the morning."

I had thought Sheila was a pain in the ass, but now I realized how wrong I'd been. She still had morals and was nice. These girls were ruthless, and I began to understand why Cole had warned me a few minutes ago.

Jordan glanced at me once more with pure hatred. "Fine, but this isn't over."

Great, already had an enemy, and I hadn't been here for

... wait, how long had I been here. I wasn't entirely sure since I'd blacked out.

"Come on, Ravey." Cole released his grip from my waist and took my hand. "Let's get out of here." He walked over to the elevators and pushed the up button.

The elevator immediately dinged, and the doors opened. We both moved inside. Once the door was closed, he pushed the number seven and turned toward me. "I'm sorry about them."

"It's not your fault." I wanted to ask a question but wasn't sure I could handle the answer. "Why did they have a red ring to their eyes?"

"You really haven't been around other paranormals, have you?" The Cole I'd met was back now. A small smirk sat on his face, and his body was relaxed.

"No, I haven't. That thought hadn't even occurred to me till now." Granted, I knew the basics but never had real-world experience. Our pack back home was close-knit. Somehow, even though my parents had been outsiders, they were welcomed with open arms. Apparently, our family was the first outsiders the pack had ever accepted.

"Well, luckily you've found an ally with me." He winked and waved both of his hands with his pointer finger out in my direction.

"Please, never do that again." I couldn't help but giggle a little. Cole seemed sincere, and for some reason, I felt like I could trust him. "But really, will you answer my question?"

"It's because she was feeding." He leaned on the door and rested his head. "Whenever a vampire feeds and shortly thereafter, the red ring is the tell."

Okay, that made sense. They both had been drinking from blood bags. "Got it."

The elevator dinged, and the doors slid open. "Come

on, your room is this way." He stepped out in front and went to the right. "We got you rooming with someone trustworthy."

For some reason, I trusted him. "Thanks. I need all the friends I can find."

"I will warn you she is slightly different." Cole stopped at the door on the right which was labeled 716. "But both Isadora and I thought this would be the best placement for the both of you."

Great. *Here's hoping that she won't attack me.*

He knocked on the door and then placed a key in the lock, turning the knob. The door swung open, and he reached in, turning on the lights.

A large couch and television were placed in the center between the openings to two hallways. Right across from the room was a decent sized kitchen that included a table for four.

"Holy crap. I was thinking this would be more like a university dorm." This place appeared to be a luxury style apartment instead of a dormitory.

"Remember the cream of the crop of the supernatural worlds attend this school." Cole entered the room and plopped himself on the black leather sofa. "Don't get me wrong ... your classes and training will be horrendous, but we get to live in luxury."

I glanced down the hallway that was closest to the door. It had a door on the right, and at the end was a bathroom. "So we don't even have to share showers with the whole floor?"

"You don't even have to share with your roommate either." He stood and motioned for me to follow him down the hallway. He stopped at the first doorway and opened it. "This is your room."

The room was twice as big as the one I had back home. There was a queen bed sitting in the middle with a teal comforter on top. The room had a walk-in closet to the right. I even had a chest of drawers and a dresser. "This is huge, and teal is my favorite color." I couldn't stop myself from going to the closet and opening it up. There were clothes that I'd never seen before hanging in there.

"The closet is full." I flipped on the light and took note of all the various button-down shirts, plaid skirts, a few pairs of jeans, and comfortable shirts.

"Remember me telling you that we didn't need to go by your house." Cole stepped into the room and placed his hands in his jean pockets. "This is why."

I looked at the labels, and they were exactly my size. "But how is this possible?"

"We have our ways." He shrugged and glanced around. "Do you like it?"

"I love it." Even the jeans and shirts were name brands. "But it still blows my mind."

"Once the headmaster locates you, she knows certain things. She knows your favorite colors, and I was able to size you up when meeting you at the baseball game. It's one of my party tricks."

"That's not very comforting." Even though I shouldn't have been all that surprised at people's abilities anymore.

"Oh, come on." Cole ran a hand over my comforter and smiled. "It's not that bad."

"Says the creeper that sized me up." It was strange that in such a short time, I'd become comfortable with Cole. I just hoped it didn't change now that I was attending the school.

"Stop." Cole chuckled and pointed at me. "Now let's go

check out your bathroom and see if we can find your new roommate."

The bathroom part sounded fun, but I wasn't excited about meeting my roommate after my last two encounters with students. That girl kissing Rage flashed through my head. My wolf growled at the sight, and I had no clue why.

"Earth to Ravey." Cole waved his hand in front of my face.

"Sorry, I zoned out." I had to get my act together and fast. I took a deep breath and forced a smile on my face. "Let's do this."

"Okay, stop." Cole laughed and rubbed a hand down his face. "Your face is kinda scary, so maybe you need a few more minutes before meeting her."

"Jackass." I stuck my tongue out at him and then forced an even cheesier smile. "I'll have you know this look works all the time."

"Probably because they're too scared to move quickly and run." He lifted both hands in surrender. "Just please, don't hurt me."

My smile fell, and my mind went straight to the bear incident. "Did I hurt the bear?"

"He's fine." Cole walked up to the door and opened it. "Let's go meet your roommate. That should liven things up."

I wasn't going to get anything out of him, so I decided I may as well suck it up and move on. "Alright." I marched out the door and back toward the den.

"Once you get settled in, you'll feel a lot better." Cole walked past me and stepped into the other hallway. "Jess, are you here?"

"Cole?" A musical voice answered him. "Is she here?"

A door opened, and Jess ran down the hallway. She

skidded into the room, and her purple eyes landed on me. "You must be Raven."

"Yes." I couldn't help my short response. This girl was mesmerizing. Her long ash blonde hair cascaded down her back, and she wore a small teal tank top with yoga pants.

"It is a little overwhelming, but don't worry. You'll get the hang of it in time." Her pink lips spread into a smile, and light reflected off of her small diamond nose piercing.

"She's already run into Jordan and Madison." Cole arched an eyebrow and shook his head.

"I hate those bitches, but at least I didn't date one of them." She tilted her head and sauntered up to Cole.

It wasn't 'til then that I realized just how short she was. She only came up to Cole's shoulders, and I was at least a head taller than her. "Really ... You dated one of them?"

"Dated is a strong word." Cole cringed and glanced down at the ground. "It was more of a Netflix and chill sort of deal."

"Wow, look who found some manners while they were gone." Jess giggled, which sounded like bells ringing.

"What are you?" The words left my mouth before I could stop them.

"I like her." She tilted her head again and turned to face me. "First off, what do I smell like to you?"

This must be some sort of trick, but what did I have to lose? "You smell like sunshine and rain." It was an odd combination.

"I always like knowing what I smell like to others." She headed into the kitchen and called over her shoulder. "I'm fae."

"Oh, so you smell differently to everyone?" That very idea was beyond my comprehension. Everyone had their own unique smell, so that didn't seem plausible.

"No, but that confirmed what I thought." She grabbed a bottle of water and twisted the lid off. "You don't feel supernatural to me, so it's odd."

"Well, I assure you I am." Although at this point, I didn't have a handle on my wolf. I wasn't sure what it all meant. "I hate to do this, but I've gotta get some rest. I'm beat."

Cole came over and wrapped me in a big, warm hug, and his cotton candy scent was comforting. "Of course, I'm beat too. So, I'll head on out." He turned and saluted Jess. "Bye."

Both Jess and I watched Cole walk out the door. When the door clicked shut, she nodded in my direction. "Get some sleep. You're going to need it for tomorrow." She winked at me and headed back to her room.

Was that some kind of warning, or was she just being kind? At this point, I wasn't sure of anything.

CHAPTER EIGHT

A knock on the door jarred me awake. "Hey, you up?" Jess's feminine voice called from behind the door.

"No, but I am now." I glanced around, getting my bearings straight.

"Get your uniform on, and get your ass out here. We're going to miss breakfast." The door opened, and Jess came barreling into the room.

This had to be some kind of weird dream. *Would someone I barely know just invite herself into my room?* I pinched myself, which made me flinch. Ouch. That hurt.

She walked into my closet, and the sound of clothes hangers clanging against the metal shelving infiltrated my ears. "Are you needing to borrow something?"

"Uh, no." She stepped out of the closet with a white button-down shirt that tied at the bottom and a red plaid uniform. "You've got to wear something acceptable but still show a little skin." She threw the items on my bed. "Here, put these on."

My blurry eyes seemed to focus and noticed that she had on a gray shirt with the same skirt. "Go put these on and get ready. I'm getting hangry, which is not good for either one of us."

For some reason, the thought of her angry scared me. The super nice ones were able to flip a whole one-eighty if the situation presented itself. "Yes, ma'am." I grabbed the clothes and headed for the bathroom.

It took me by surprise that everything I needed seemed to be there. My favorite jasmine shampoo was in the shower along with my usual makeup. I jumped into the shower, washing quickly and dried off. Within minutes, I was dressed and ready. I put on my favorite pink lipstick and fluffed my hair so it had a little volume. The humidity would make it limp within seconds otherwise.

Jess was waiting for me in the den. "Thank God, I think I'm turning into Betty White. This may be a snickers type of emergency."

"Let's go. We can't have that." I restrained myself from laughing ... just barely.

We hurried down the hallway, and she punched the elevator button. "So, you're already going to be on Jordan's bad side. Be ready for it. Vampire-wise, she's the head bitch in control."

"Wait. Why would I be on her bad side?" Even though I figured as much, having it confirmed made my insides cold.

"It's all because of Cole and how he treats you." Jess spelled it out for me just as the door opened.

That didn't make any sense. I followed behind her and leaned against the elevator wall. Somehow, we were the only two people inside. "How is that my fault?"

"There are three men here that any girl would die to have." She held three fingers up and touched each one as she named them. "Cole, Rage, and Damien. They started the Academy at about the same time and have been here three years. They haven't left this place yet because of how much value they bring Isadora. When another group comes along that can help in the way they can, they'll head off to their own graduation."

"Okay." Still, it didn't make any sense to me, but at least I knew the guys were around twenty-one.

"Rage has been in a *relationship* for a year, and the girl, Ashley, would cut any bitch that gets close to him. He's only using her for one thing. I still don't know why he picked her, but he didn't ask my opinion." She sighed dramatically and rolled her eyes. "So that really just leaves Cole and Damien up for grabs."

My wolf whimpered, and I forced my face to remain indifferent. "Well, fated mates are nonexistent these days."

"That's not true. They are rare, but not impossible." The elevator opened, and she stepped out before turning to me. "Are you okay? You kinda look like you might need to take a dump or something."

Great, right when I thought I was being smooth and unreadable, I look constipated. "No, sorry. Was thinking about something."

"Girl, we need to work on your thinking face." She sighed and shook her head. "Anywho, all three guys are jackasses. Only makes them even more dreamy, and Isadora has taken to them."

"So, I've met Cole and Rage, but what's Damien like?" I had to get my mind off of focusing on Rage and that girl.

"Damien is kind of a loner, and he'll only really associate with Rage and Cole." A small smile spread across her face, and her cheeks turned rosy. "He's a bear shifter so …"

Jess was still talking, but I couldn't focus on her words

any longer. I attacked a bear last night. Could that have been him? Did I hurt Cole and Rage's best friend?

"We've got to work on your zoning out thing." Jess opened the door and motioned for me to walk in.

"I'm sorry. Everything is still a little weird for me." I stepped outside, and the warm sun hit my skin. It rejuvenated me a little bit. I was determined to grab Cole and make him tell me everything.

"I get that. It's hard taking all this in." We moved along the sidewalk that connected the dorms to the main building. "Hell, let's be real. I'm still not acclimated, not really, and I've been here a year."

That was hard to believe. Jess was nice, gorgeous, and sweet. "Well, if you aren't, then there is no telling if I'll ever be."

"Not everyone is welcoming and accepting." Her face dropped a little, but she shook it off and flipped her hair over her shoulder. "Enough of me being a Debbie Downer."

We entered through the set of double doors that led us into a modern connection between the main building and the cafeteria. The connector was all glass, and I glanced through, noting there were several tables and chairs. Students were scattered throughout with open books.

As soon as we made our way inside, the smell of bacon and eggs made my stomach grumble.

"Come on, we'll grab some food up here." Jess motioned for me to follow her to the middle of the cafeteria. "Let's get it before they start packing up."

My eyes were so focused on the food that I didn't even see Jordan. She stuck out her foot right as I was taking a step, and I fell to the ground hard.

"For a wolf shifter, you are pretty damn clumsy." She giggled and glanced at Madison next to her. "And she did that right in front of Cole. Obviously, she has no class, and that's why they stuck her with the pathetic excuse for a fae."

My wolf growled and began forcing herself forward. "I could see why you'd need to trip others and put them down. That's the only way your fake ass will ever get somewhere."

The cafeteria became silent as Jordan's chest heaved each time she took a breath. "You stupid bitch! Don't make me show everyone how easy it would be to bring you to the brink of death."

I refused to give her any more ammo or even react to her words. However, I felt a pair of eyes burning into my backside.

"Are you proud of yourself now?" Cole's voice was cold with an edge to his words.

At first, I thought he was talking to me until I saw his eyes were glued on Jordan.

"It's best she learns where she is in the pecking order." Jordan smiled at Cole and licked her bottom lip.

"Which pecking order would that be?" He tilted his head and crossed his arms. "Would it be the biggest bitch or the most manipulative heartless bitch?"

"Are you being serious right now?" The normal golden hue of her eyes seemed to darken. "She's a fucking newbie, who obviously has issues with her wolf."

How the hell did she know that? It seemed as if I had my issues plastered on my forehead. "If you want to pick on me, fine, but leave Jess out of it."

Something flickered in Cole's eyes. "You best leave Ravey alone, or you'll have to answer to me."

Jordan's mouth dropped open, and she kind of looked like a fish out of water the way she was opening and closing it.

"Come on, Jordan." Madison grabbed her arm and tugged her toward the door to leave. "They aren't worth it."

Both girls walked out the cafeteria door, slamming it in their wake.

A big grin spread across Jess's face. "You took her head-on and on your first day."

"Don't encourage her." Cole chuckled and grabbed my arm, pulling me in the direction of Rage and another guy.

"Hey, I want breakfast." Besides, I didn't want to be around Rage, especially now that I knew he's got a girlfriend.

"Don't worry about that." He stopped at a random table and looked at the guy sitting there. "Go get her breakfast. Get her one of everything."

The guy nodded his head and stood.

I glanced at him. "You don't …"

A hand reached around me and covered my mouth. "Ignore her, and bring it to us."

That bastard had some nerve cutting me off. I opened my mouth and bit down on two of his fingers.

"Now, now." Cole chuckled, and his breath hit my ear. "I'm all for that kind of foreplay. I just didn't realize you were one for PDA."

A drop of his blood fell into my mouth. Somehow, the taste was sweeter than chocolate and even more delicious. Surprisingly, I wanted more.

"Damnit." He pulled his hand away and shook his head. "You're going to be the death of me."

Shit. I can't believe that I did that. However, I wasn't going to admit it was an accident in front of him. "Good. Don't ever try to keep me quiet."

A devilish grin crossed his face. "Maybe I like it loud."

Oh, dear God. Did he turn everything into a dirty innuendo? I glanced around and realized that the guy was already putting food on plates for me.

"Come on, Ravey." He tugged on my arm and led me to the table. There was only one extra chair there, and it just had to be between Damien and Cole. Or at least I was assuming that he was the bear shifter.

The guy had some gauze on his shoulders that peeked out from his white polo shirt, and his dark, gray eyes examined me. He was built similar to Rage but looked like an MMA fighter. He ran his fingers through his short auburn hair.

"Hi, I'm Ra ..."

"I know who you are." He held my gaze as he grabbed his orange juice and took a long sip.

Okay, this was going great. I took my seat, which had me directly facing Rage. My body began to betray me, and I held my breath. The last thing I needed was his earthy scent causing me to be even more confused than I already was.

"Do you know how to stay out of trouble?" Rage leaned back in his seat and crossed his arms.

"No, I don't." There was no reason to lie to him. I gained nothing from his dislike.

Cole reached over and put an arm around me, glancing at Damien. "See, she's straight-up honest."

"Yeah, but dangerous." Damien snorted and shook his head. "She doesn't have a hold on her wolf at all."

"You're just pissed because she whooped your ass." Cole pointed at Damien and placed an elbow on the table. "I mean, you really didn't have a chance."

"Shut the fuck up." Damien stood and growled. He grabbed his tray off the table and walked toward the exit. "I'll meet you outside in fifteen. Don't be late."

As he sauntered off, the guy who grabbed my food set

down three plates in front of me. I couldn't believe my eyes. He brought me an entire plate of bacon and sausage, another plate of French toast and pancakes, and the last plate had a mound of eggs with cheese. I wasn't sure how I was going to eat one full plate, but there wasn't any way I could let it all go to waste. "Thanks."

"Anytime." The guy smiled and winked at me. "Enjoy."

He was cute with chestnut hair and almond eyes.

"Now scram." Rage waved the guy off, and his charcoal eyes held me in place. "You better eat."

As Jess peeled away from the buffet line, she glanced around for a place to sit.

I figured she was coming to sit with us, but she passed by us, heading to an empty table.

"We have an open seat here." I pointed to the seat that Damien had vacated.

"No, we don't." Rage lifted his feet and placed them in the chair. "Keep going."

That definitely wasn't going to happen. "Yes, we do." I reached over and grabbed the chair, pulling it closer to me and making his feet drop. "Come sit next to me."

"Uh ..." Jess bit her bottom lip. She looked at me and then back at Rage. "I'm going to go over here instead."

"I'll go with you." I stood and reached down, lifting my overflowing tray.

"No, you stay." Rage's jaw twitched as he watched. "You're welcome here. She isn't."

The girl from last night entered the cafeteria and headed in our direction. Her forehead was creased, and she scanned me up and down. "Hey, baby."

Rage ignored her as he kept his eyes locked on me. "I said sit."

"You heard the man." Cole's face had a huge smile on it,

and I swore he would've been eating popcorn if there was any around.

"Shut up, Cole." Both Rage and I yelled at him together.

"What's going on here?" Ashley placed her hand on the seat I'd just vacated.

"Sorry, we're all full here." Cole pointed at the chair Rage had his feet on and the vacant one next to him. "This is Ravey's seat. You heard the man."

"You've got to be kidding me." Ashley took a step back, and her mouth dropped open.

This whole situation was strange, and for some damn reason, I wanted to listen to Rage. However, Jess had been sweet to me and seemed like she could be a good friend. "They are. They were saving this seat for you." I forced a smile at the hussy and turned to walk away. "Come on, let's go find another table."

As we made our way to another table, it was obvious how quiet the other three had become. That was until Cole cleared his throat, and ice laced his voice once more. "How does it feel to be given the seat by a newbie?"

I cringed. Cole was blatantly antagonizing her. I didn't need another enemy so soon.

"Girl, I can't believe you." Jess rushed to an open table and set down her food. "You turned down one of them after you got invited to their table."

"That's not a big deal." I was really uncomfortable with the attention and just wanted to eat.

"No one outside their little tribe has ever been invited to their table. Ashley has sat there only a handful of times, but Rage never requested it." She took a bite of her French toast that was somehow swimming in syrup. "I've never seen Rage act that way."

Ashley leaned in and was talking to Rage, but his face

remained emotionless. Eventually, he stood and took a few steps our way.

"Are you fucking serious right now?" Ashley's face almost matched her hair color perfectly. Somehow it turned even darker as Rage ignored her. She picked up the tray he had left and slammed it on the table. "You're even leaving your fucking trash."

He stopped when he reached our table, and his eyes locked on me. He turned his head to address Ashley. "If it bothers you that badly, then you throw it away." His tone was harsh, and he stood rigid in front of me.

"Oh, here, take mine too." Cole jumped up from the table and saluted me as he exited the room.

Rage pointed to my food and sighed. "Hurry and eat up. Damien will be pissed if you don't arrive on time."

"What?" I had assumed he had been talking to him and Cole. "Me?"

"Yes, he's the one training you today." He turned on his heels and walked out the door.

"This year might be fun with you here." Jess giggled and began stuffing her face with food.

She was thinking about having a good year whereas I wasn't sure I was going to last through the end of the day. This was Damien's chance to kick my ass after what I did to him last night.

CHAPTER NINE

All the food that I'd eaten was sitting hard on my stomach. Had I known I was going to be training with Damien, I wouldn't have stuffed myself. At least I hadn't finished that last plate ... not completely.

Jess had wanted to go with me outside, but I shooed her on. She didn't need to be late for her training either.

Damien was waiting at the edge of the clearing. He sat on a stone bench and leaned back with his eyes closed, enjoying the faint breeze that ruffled his short hair. He was hot as hell when he wasn't being so guarded.

The breeze blew in the opposite direction, causing him to stiffen and glance in my direction. "It's about time."

He was full of shit, but I wouldn't call him on it. In his defense, I did attack him last night, and he hadn't hurt me. I owed him one.

After a moment, he stood and began walking toward the woods.

If he thought the silent treatment was going to work on me, it wouldn't. I was used to being invisible.

I hurried and followed behind him despite how fast he

was going. It was obvious he knew this area. He didn't slow down, so I had to keep pace. I hated to call up my wolf, but now was a time that I needed her.

She sprang forward just enough without forcing the change. When she realized I wasn't going to yank her back, she lent me her vision and agility.

The woods smelled of water and flowers. Even though summer was only a few weeks away, the flowers still smelled as if they had just bloomed.

After several minutes, Damien slowed as a clearing appeared ahead. The grass was longer, and dandelions were scattered throughout. I was a little odd because unlike most people, I firmly believed that they were good omens. I'd let that secret slip to Greg once, and he laughed at me. He had told me that was ridiculous and they were just weeds. However, to me, I associated them with freedom. Usually, they only occurred where most people didn't venture and where I could be myself, unafraid of judgment.

"I was surprised you did that well." His voice caught me off-guard since it'd been a while since he last spoke to me.

If he was looking for a reaction, I wasn't going to oblige him. I stood there, waiting for him to go on. Most people liked to talk. They underrated the power of observation and just keeping their damn mouths shut. Obviously, he was wanting me to ask what he meant.

It felt a little like we were having a standoff, but I refused to be the one who cracked first.

"Now, I want you to close your eyes. Tell me what you hear and sense." He arched an eyebrow, as if he was daring me to argue.

In all transparency, I wanted to, but I wouldn't back down since that's what he wanted. So instead, I took a deep breath and closed my eyes.

"What do you smell?" His voice was lower and seemed like a challenge.

"I smell the humidity, the flowers, and your scent ... pine and cypress." I couldn't believe that I just said that. There was definitely something wrong with my filter.

"Nothing else?" His tone was condescending.

"No, nothing else." I breathed deeply, hoping to discover something new.

"Push yourself." His voice seemed to be getting closer, and he chuckled. "I mean, that is ... if you can."

Every time a cocky male acted this way, it made me want to wipe the smug grin off his face. I allowed my wolf to surge forward a little once more. "There is a nest of eggs above me and some squirrels in the tree to my left."

"What made the difference?"

"My wolf surged forward." An honest answer, there was no reason to lie.

"See that's your problem." Damien huffed. "You think of things as you or your wolf. You should be one being, not two separate entities living in the same body. Go ahead, and open your eyes."

I had always felt like my relationship with my wolf was strange, but it was unsettling having someone else point it out.

"We've got to work on your connection. It shouldn't be your human side fighting against your wolf." He ran a hand through his hair and sighed. "So, we're going to practice merging the two."

For the next eight hours, he had me smelling and sensing things around me with my wolf at the forefront in my mind.

As I ENTERED my dorm room, I noticed Jess was on the couch. She had supernatural anatomy and basic traits books scattered all around her. She glanced at me and grinned. "How did your day go?"

"I'm exhausted." I walked over and dropped into one of the chairs beside her. "Apparently, my wolf isn't fully integrated, so we're working on that."

She reached over and shut one of her books. "I didn't see you at lunch."

"That's because I didn't have one." I leaned my head back on the seat. "I'm so exhausted."

"Well, I'm about to head out for dinner. Wanna go?" She stood and stretched out her back.

"No, I'll have to pass." I yawned and melted into my chair. "I'm sorry."

"I remember my first day." She smiled at me and opened the door. "I'll bring you back something to eat."

"Thanks." A shower was calling my name.

As the door shut, my phone dinged, alerting me to a text message. I reached down and opened it.

Hey. Call me when u can. I miss you. <3

Great, did I really have it in me to talk to Greg? Either way, I needed to check in with my parents. It had been way too late to call them when it was all said and done last night.

I dialed my parents' number and waited as the line rang. By the second ring, Mom answered. "Raven, is that you?"

"Yeah, who else were you expecting?" They had caller ID. Mom was losing it.

"Sorry, of course, it's you." She let out a sigh and cleared her throat. "We were worried when we didn't hear from you last night. How is everything going?"

"Come on, Liz," Dad spoke from the background. "Put the girl on speaker."

It sounded as if the phone was being shuffled, and then the TV in the background became clearer. "Dad, you there too?"

"Despite your mother's best efforts, I'm here." Dad chuckled, and Mom huffed.

I could picture her rolling her eyes and Dad grinning. "Well, I'm glad."

"Everything okay down there, kiddo?" Dad's voice got clearer as if he had moved closer to the phone.

"Yeah. Sorry I didn't call last night, but it was so intense." I wasn't about to tell them what happened. "I just got through my first day of training, and I'm wiped."

"Well, I'm just happy to hear your voice." Mom sniffled.

"I'm glad to talk to you too." I hadn't even realized how bad I needed to talk to them until now.

"Greg stopped by today," Dad said. "He apologized for his actions and said he felt really bad."

"He texted me earlier." The last thing I wanted to do was call him, let alone talk about him. "I wanted to call you two first."

"That's my baby girl." Pride was evident in Mom's words. "Is everyone being nice down there?"

If she only knew the truth. "My roommate is great. We seemed to have hit it off."

"That's great." I could hear the smile in Dad's voice. "Is she a shifter?"

"Uh ... No, actually she's a fae." I didn't want to give too much information away.

"What?" Mom was shocked. "They intermingle y'all?"

"I don't know about everyone else, but she and I are." I

wouldn't have wanted it any other way now. "It's working so far."

"That's good dear," Dad spoke up.

They were acting weird, but I didn't really want to analyze it. Even though it was all mind exercises today, I was completely exhausted both mentally and physically. "Guys, I hate to do this, but I'm exhausted."

"Give us a call in the next couple of days." Dad paused for a moment, and he whispered something to Mom. "We love you."

"I love you both too." I hadn't ever been away from them like this before, so it was new for all of us.

"Be careful, and call us soon." Once Mom finished the words, their line went dead.

The last thing I wanted to do was call Greg, but the longer I put it off, the worse it'd be. I pulled his name from my contacts, and my finger hovered over it. All I wanted to do was go change into my pajamas and lay in bed.

Before I did just that, I pushed his name. The line began to ring, and I hoped that he wouldn't answer. Right on the fourth ring, he picked up. "Hey."

Dammit. I thought I'd be home free. "Hi." I didn't know what to say to him and instantly regretted calling him.

"How are you?" For the first time ever, he sounded awkward and unsure of himself.

"Okay. You?" If he thought I was going to start pouring out my heart or tell him what had been going on here, he was gravely mistaken.

"Not great." A door shut, and there was a shuffling of the phone on his end. "Look, I'm sorry about yesterday."

Had it only been a day? It felt like a whole lot longer now that I thought about it. "You thought they were coming for you."

He chuckled darkly. "I just want you to know that I realized I was acting like an asshole. Maybe I could come down and visit after you get settled. I'd like to see you."

My gut reaction was to tell him 'no,' but he was trying to be sweet. "Maybe, we'll have to see how it goes."

"What are you saying?" His tone hardened.

Great, now he was getting pissy. "I'm saying that it's a lot different down here, and I don't know when I'll get settled." I didn't fit in was what I wanted to say, but I wouldn't be admitting that to him, considering how he was acting.

The distance between us felt more like worlds apart instead of just states.

"How is it?" He seemed interested in what I was saying.

"I don't know how to explain it." All the people seemed to be assholes to one another, and no one seemed to like me. I wasn't sure if Cole's interest was genuine or not. The only one I felt comfortable with was Jess.

"Well, you could try." The edge to his tone was back.

The door to our dorm room opened, and Jess came swaying in. Both hands held plates that were piled high with steak, potatoes, and a huge piece of blackberry cobbler. My stomach rumbled in anticipation.

"Girl, get off that phone, and come eat with me." Jess glided into the kitchen and set the plates on the table.

"Who's that?" Greg's voice was sullen and made him sound like he was a toddler.

"My roommate, Jess." I was ready to get off the phone. "She brought dinner to me, so I've gotta go."

"Oh, will you call me tomorrow?"

"Yeah, sure." I wanted off the phone and now.

"Love you."

"Bye." He always proclaimed his love, but his actions

didn't mirror it. I hung up the phone and walked into the kitchen.

"Who was that?" Jess pulled her plate of food in front of her.

I had to hold back a laugh. There was one large difference between her plate and mine. Her steak was cooked while mine was rare. "Sure you don't want to eat this one?" I pushed my plate toward her.

"Oh, hell no. I prefer my steak not mooing." She pointed her fork at mine and wrinkled her nose.

"Aw, then it's no good." Not able to withstand it any longer, I grabbed my fork and knife before tearing into it. When I placed the steak in my mouth, I seriously considered whether I'd died and gone to heaven.

For a few minutes, we ate in amicable silence. That was until Jess took a drink of her water and cut another piece off her steak. "How was training with Damien?"

"I'm pretty sure it was his normal." I finished the piece of food in my mouth and swallowed. "He grunted a lot, told me to do better, and even pushed me and my wolf to bond like a shifter should really be."

"Everyone is talking about how you're the first to train with Damien and how the elite Cole seems to have taken an interest in you." She pushed back from the table and grinned. "For once, people wanted to talk to me instead of their usual shunning."

If this was them taking a shine to someone, I must not have had a clue how they treated others. "Why do they shun you?"

"It's partly because I'm fae." She stared at the table and scowled. "Most of my kind stay in our world, but I wanted something different. I felt different than them, those back home." She closed her eyes and shook her head. "And because my parents aren't as rich as theirs and not very powerful."

"Why does that have anything to do with it?" Her parents weren't a reflection of her power.

"Most of the kids here were raised by powerful parents." She stabbed the blackberry cobbler and took a bite. "Their parents came here too, so they're kind of born into it."

"So, we're the outliers then." It kind of made sense that we didn't fit in; we weren't one of them.

"Exactly." She gave a sad smile and stared at the table. "So, it's kind of nice having you here. Maybe I finally have an ally."

I didn't like trusting people because I was trying to keep my wolf secrets. I did always feel like my relationship with my animal was different than others. It always felt like she was trying to overtake me while others just seemed to blend. It was odd always feeling like an outlier. That somehow you were so different that you didn't belong in any section of the bell-shaped curve. However, here, they already knew my secret, and it was a little unnerving. "You know, that sounds nice."

She glanced up and met my eyes. "Really?"

"Girl, if I was trying to keep my distance from you … I've been doing a shit job, right?" If I was being truthful with myself, I'd already known that she and I were destined to be friends. I reached across the table with my right hand. "Friends?"

Her eyes sparked, and she grabbed my hand. "Friends."

"Okay, now that we got that out of the way, I'm going to finish up here and go to bed." My arms were getting heavy, and I swore my legs felt like they weighed a ton.

"Alright, I'll leave you to it." She stood and stretched her back. "I'm going to go take a hot shower."

That did sound amazing. "Go on, I'm almost done here anyway."

She grabbed her dish and cup, placing them in the sink before heading to her room.

The blackberry cobbler was to die for. I wasn't sure if the steak or cobbler was the best. I finished shoveling my food into my mouth and stood. It seemed that the food gave me a little more energy, and the full moon tugged on me.

I thought maybe a walk by myself would calm me so I could sleep better afterward. I grabbed my keys and locked the door behind me. Within minutes, I was outside underneath the full moon. My wolf whimpered inside of me. She wanted to run. Although, I honestly didn't think I had the strength to change.

I headed in the direction that Damien and I had trained earlier. I bet that would be a good relaxing place to stare at the moon. I took my time strolling through the woods, unlike earlier. Lightning bugs were out and flying around everywhere, their flashes lighting up the woods all around them.

It didn't take long to find the path to the clearing, but I hadn't been prepared to not be alone. There, in the middle of the field, sat someone. An earthy scent filled my nose. My stomach dropped when I realized who it was.

Before Rage could sense me, I turned to make my way back toward the dorms. Still, as soon as I took my first step in retreat, his dark, raspy voice called out. "What are you doing here?"

Shit. He had to be talking to me because there wasn't another person around. I tried to be sneaky and take another step away from him. Instead, he turned around with his eyes locking on me.

Okay, so retreat wasn't an option. Butterflies seemed to take flight in my belly, and my heart rate kicked up. We'd never been alone together before and now we were both out in the woods. I just hoped something bad wasn't going to happen.

CHAPTER TEN

If I hadn't thought he was gorgeous before, there would be no way I could deny it now. In the moonlight, his chocolate eyes appeared to become black, and he wore a thin t-shirt that somehow defined his muscles even more than before. At the bottom of his sleeve, the edge of a tattoo peeked out.

I wanted to go over there and lift his sleeve higher so I could see the entire pattern. Honestly, pressing my body against him didn't sound so bad either.

"Are you just going to stare at me, or do you plan on answering any time soon?" He scanned his eyes up and down my body.

Damn, I was in over my head. I'd never been this attracted to someone back home. Greg was cute, but no Rage. "I didn't expect anyone to be here."

"Damien brought you here to train earlier." I wasn't sure whether that was a question or statement from him.

"Yes, he did." I had no clue what to say to this guy. He had someone he ... No, I refused to let my mind go there. Just the thought made me want to heave.

"Your scent is fucking everywhere." His voice sounded almost pained. "Why aren't you at the dorm or out running?"

"I needed to get away and didn't trust myself to shift." The words were out before I could take them back. Honesty probably wasn't the best policy when it came to him.

He huffed and stood. "Of course you are."

"What is that supposed to mean?" He may treat everyone like this, but it wouldn't work on me.

"Not in tune with your wolf." Even though his hair was short, he ran his fingers through it. "It's driving me crazy."

"It's driving you crazy?" There was no way he could be serious. "I'm so sorry that I'm inconveniencing you." I couldn't help the sarcasm dripping from each word.

"Ugh, that's not what I meant." He blew out a harsh breath.

It was strange because every time I saw Rage, I wasn't sure whether I wanted to jump him or slap him. "Why aren't you out running?"

"I don't trust myself yet." He drew nearer to me, and his eyes landed on my lips.

My tongue darted out, licking them, and I wondered what he would taste like.

"Well, well." Cole's boisterous voice cut through the tension. "What do we have here?"

Rage jerked away from me like a bad habit. "It's about time you jackasses finally got here."

"It sure seemed to me like we interrupted something." Cole stepped into the clearing with Damien right beside him.

"I was just leaving." I really didn't want to deal with them at that moment. I only went for a walk to be alone and clear my head. Not be with Rage and get even more confused.

"No, Ravey." Cole pouted and headed over, grabbing my hand.

A heavy growl resonated from deep inside Rage as his eyes zoned in on our hands.

"Maybe you should let her go." Damien placed himself in between Cole and Rage. "Did you invite Ashley to meet us here too?"

Her name was like an instant cold shower. He had someone, and so did I. There wasn't anything between us, and allowing myself to be weak would only get me hurt.

"No, I'd never bring her here." Rage flinched backward, increasing the distance between us.

There was an awkward silence that descended around us. "I needed to get out for a while and probably should be heading back. Jess will be worried about me."

"You do need your rest." It felt like Damien was really inspecting me. "You had a hard day today. Tomorrow, you'll attend the supernatural cultures class, so you'll get a day's break."

"That class is horrible but interesting." Cole seemed to glow in the moonlight. "But it's important stuff. Do you need me to walk you home?"

"I'm fine, but thanks." I wanted to get away—escape. "Have fun tonight." I wanted to add 'not too much fun,' but I bit my tongue.

I glanced at Rage one last time and made myself turn away. Staying here would only make things worse.

As I entered the cafeteria with Jess the next morning, my appetite just about vanished when I saw Ashley sitting with the guys. From what it had sounded like, she didn't get to do that regularly, so it took me by surprise.

Her hair was piled in a messy bun with strands cascading around her face. She was leaning into Rage with a huge smile on her face, but the guys were sitting there, barely speaking a word to one another.

"Why is she sitting with them?" Jess frowned and slowed her pace.

"No clue." I didn't want to talk about it. Although, the more I saw her practically sitting in Rage's lap, the more I wanted to puke or throw a tantrum. Even though I had no claim on him.

Forcing myself to remain calm, I grabbed a plate and began piling on the food. There were eggs, bacon, Belgian waffles, and all kinds of fruit. I thought maybe I could eat away my feelings.

Jess remained quiet as she fixed her plate too, and we finished around the same time.

There was a vacant table on the other side of the cafeteria from the guys, so I nodded in that direction. "Let's sit there."

"But Cole is waving at you." Jess's forehead creased, but she followed me as I walked over to the table.

"I don't really care." That was partly true, so I wasn't lying. I couldn't be over there, not with Ashley and Rage. I didn't need any other people seeming to target me. I already had the vampire princess pissed. At this very moment, Jordan was staring at me with pure hatred.

Even though my appetite was still gone, I grabbed my fork and shoveled a large amount of eggs on it. There was no telling what might happen today, so I needed to fuel up.

"I'm sorry about Rage." Jess dropped her voice, and she frowned.

Oh, hell no. "There isn't anything to be sorry about." I took a bite of eggs, but that didn't prevent me from talking. "He's an ass, and they are a match made in heaven. It doesn't phase me. Anyway, I have a boyfriend."

"You haven't dumped that loser yet?" Cole rolled his eyes and dropped into one of the vacant seats between Jess and me.

"We've been together since we were sixteen." I lifted my fork with another pile of eggs on it and ate the large bite. "It's not like three days were going to change that."

"It's kind of hard to believe that you've only been here three days." Cole wiggled his eyebrows. "You've already got two sets of enemies. Not to mention messing around with one of my best friends. You're the missing link I've been searching for."

"First off, I'm not messing around with anyone." Why did everyone think Rage and I had something between us? We didn't. It was just mutual dislike. "Secondly, the reason why I have one set of enemies is sitting right here." I pointed at him sitting at our table.

Cole placed his elbows on the table and propped his head in his hands. "Oh, please. Tell me more."

"You're such an ass." I grabbed a piece of bacon and twirled it around like it was a weapon. "Learn some manners." I crammed the whole piece in my mouth.

"You know, you're right." Smirking, he leaned back in his seat and pointed to me. "Obviously, I should be learning etiquette from you."

Jess exploded into giggles until I glared at her, and then she mashed her lips together. "I'm sorry, but he's kind of on-point right now ... with you."

"Traitor." I grabbed a napkin and wiped the grease from my fingers. "Who is my second set of enemies?"

"Ashley." A smirk crossed his face. "What are you going to do about it?"

"Why in the world would she be mad at me?" I haven't done anything for her to be upset. Sure, Rage was hot, but it wasn't like I was publicly acknowledging it.

"Because Rage has taken more notice of you than he ever has of her." He turned his body around and tilted his head toward their table.

There sat Ashley talking to Rage, but he was glancing off in another direction, not even pretending to pay attention.

"Can you stop talking?" Damien grumbled, but the words were clear to everyone in the cafeteria.

"What?" Ashley flinched at the words, and her mouth dropped open.

"Do you not understand English?" Damien stood, and the cafeteria silenced. "I said shut the fuck up."

"You can't talk to me like that." Ashley glanced at Rage and grabbed his arm. "Tell him."

He yanked his arm out of her grasp. "I'm not telling him shit. I agree." He lifted his head and scowled. "You're just over here blabbing, and we don't want to hear it."

"Are you being serious right now?" Her voice turned into a shriek, and her hands began to shake. "You asked me to sit here."

"No, actually, I didn't." He stood and crossed his arms. "You sat down, and I didn't even want to waste the energy to tell you to leave. Don't make it out to be something more than it is."

"That's bull shit, and you know it." Ashley's gaze landed squarely on me.

"Oh ... now, this is going to be fun." Cole winked at me and turned back to focus his attention on her. "You miss me, eh?"

"I wasn't even looking at you." Her face began to turn a shade of red. I wasn't sure if it was from anger or embarrassment. Maybe it was safe to say it was the combination of both.

"It's okay to admit it." He acted as if he was flipping his hair over his shoulder. "I'm pretty hot."

"This isn't some type of game, Cole." She pointed her finger in my direction. "That bitch hasn't even been here a week, and she's already screwing shit up."

"What exactly is she screwing up?" Jess's violet eyes glowed, and she glared at Ashley.

I couldn't believe that both Jess and Cole were standing up for me.

"They've all been different since she's gotten here." She stomped her foot and clenched her hands. "She needs to crawl back into whatever hole she crawled out of."

"So, you're saying Rage has been acting indifferent to you?" There was a challenge in Cole's eyes.

"Yes, and she's the only variable that changed." She shook her head, causing her hair to bounce behind her.

"Is that how you're justifying it in your head?" Cole's dark laugh seemed to echo across the cafeteria.

"Let me make it clear. Obviously, I've needed to do this for a while." Rage grabbed her arm and pulled her hard toward him.

Her breathing increased, and a small smile spread across her face. "Yeah, baby?"

This was going to be bad. I wasn't sure why she was smiling, but I had a feeling he was about to pull the rug out from under her.

"First off, don't 'baby' me." His eyes were now slits, and there was a tick in his jaw. "You're nothing to me."

"What?" She took a deep breath and shook her head no. "That's not true."

"Yes, it is." He let her go and took several large steps away so he was next to Damien, who had been silent the entire time. He quieted his voice so only the table could hear. "You were just a distraction and nothing more. I told you from the very beginning that you were a mere distraction; just a way for me to pass time."

"But it changed." Tears welled in her eyes, and it sounded as if she was begging.

A part of me felt bad for her, but these guys didn't seem to put on charades. She should've known what she was getting into.

"No, I allowed you to think it was something." He chuckled, and a smirk spread across his face. He whispered, "But now I need to fix my mistake. You were always a distraction. You will always be just another notch in my belt."

"You asshole!" She spun away from him, and her eyes met mine. "You'll pay for this."

Right when I was beginning to feel bad for her, she had to go and do that.

"Misplaced blame is only for the ignorant." The words came out before I could stop them. "So, I'm not surprised by your words."

Cole began laughing hard and placed an arm around my shoulders. "God, I love you."

"This isn't over." Ashley's face was the same color as a tomato, and a tear ran down her cheek, leaving a wet trail behind.

"Come on, Ashley." Jordan and Madison appeared

beside her. "Let's get you away from this slut and her fairy trash."

"I'm not a fairy." Jess wiggled her fingers, and the water from both her and my cups jumped out, splashing all over the three girls. They were now standing there with their clothes dripping wet and in a puddle.

"Both of you are going to pay for this." Jordan marched to the cafeteria door and held it open as the other two girls ran through.

"That was epic." Cole chuckled and dropped his arm. "Jess, we may have underrated you."

"It's just nice to have a friend." She focused on me with a smile.

"Ravey, things sure are getting interesting with you around." Cole bumped his shoulder into mine.

"I'm sorry about that," Rage said as he and Damien reached our table.

"You don't need to apologize to me." Cole smiled, placing a hand on his chest where his heart should have been beating. "But thank you for your kind words and concern for my well-being."

"You're such an idiot sometimes." Damien punched Cole in the arm.

"Now that's not a way to get into my pants." Cole tsked and rubbed his arm.

"Good, I'm trying to do everything possible to not get in there." Damien glanced at his watch and began moving away. "Remember, Raven, we'll be continuing our training sessions every Monday, Wednesday, and Friday until you get a handle on things."

Like I could have forgotten that, but at that moment, my priority was getting away from Rage. "I don't even know where my classroom is, so I better get going."

"I'm sure someone here would love to help you." Cole's smile seemed to fill his whole face.

"Yeah, Jess said she would help me earlier." So that was a lie, but this was a serious test of our friendship. If she didn't get the hint, I could very possibly wind up killing her.

"Can't let my girl get lost." Jess stood and waited on me. "Let's go so we both aren't late."

Not needing any additional encouragement, I stood and rushed to the trash bins. I didn't even bother saying 'Bye' to any of the guys. For now, I had to get distance from them even though a part of me didn't want to go. It had everything to do with Rage, and that wasn't cool. My whole life, I had never wanted a guy to have that much influence on me. I wanted to be my own person, whoever that was. At the moment though, the wolf part of me was ecstatic about the scene that had just gone down. I had to keep my head on straight. I didn't need enemies and didn't need to be a target. Not even a week here, and I already had two sets of people that hated my guts. I didn't need to be anyone else's target. I needed to lay low and hopefully keep my wolf in check. It was going to be an even bigger struggle since they wanted me to let her free and become more of a part of me.

CHAPTER ELEVEN

As I entered the classroom, I was surprised to see how many other students were inside. There were eleven other kids already seated. For some reason, I figured that I would be the only one there, but in hindsight, I realized that didn't make sense.

There were three rows of desks, and the back of the room was already filled. There was only a desk in the front middle section that was vacant. I guessed that one would be mine.

I headed in that direction when one of the kids stuck out her foot, trying to trip me. Luckily, I managed to dodge it but at the amusement of over half the class.

The girl leaned over, her sickening sweet smell hitting my nose. "That's what you get for bothering Jordan."

Of course, she was a vampire. Even if she didn't smell like one, her pale skin and sharp features would have alerted me. Not wanting to cause even more problems, I ignored her and sat in the open seat, which happened to be right next to her. My first class was already starting out great.

"Why don't you go back home and relieve us from all our misery?" The girl on the other side of me frowned and leaned away from me.

That one burned a little. She was another wolf shifter like me, and she was acting that way. Out of everyone here, I thought she'd be a little nicer to me. I forced myself to look forward and remain emotionless.

Thankfully, an older man, who had to be in his early to mid-forties, entered the room. He wore all black, and his dark hair was trimmed short. He smelled of herbs and lavender. "Is there a problem here?"

No one in the room answered.

His gaze landed on me, and he tilted his head. "You must be Raven." He strolled to the middle of the room and gazed around. "Did anyone bother you, Miss Wright?"

Yeah, I wasn't going to be falling for this. If I ratted out anyone, it would just get worse for me. "No, not at all."

He arched an eyebrow and glanced at each student, one by one. "Anyone else have a different answer?"

Once again, the room remained silent. After a few seconds, the man sighed and nodded his head. "Very well." He walked over to me and smiled. "Miss Wright, I'm so happy that you are joining our class. I'm Professor Shaw and will be your teacher." His gaze landed straight on my necklace. "Fortunately, this class just started last week, so you haven't missed much. This is one class that begins each summer and ends when I feel like each person is ready to move on to the next level."

At least, I hadn't missed too much. Any small victory was a big win for me at this point.

"Now, let's jump right into it." He turned and wrote 'vampires' on the whiteboard in black. "One of the most important things every good leader knows is how each supernatural race's beliefs, customs, and leadership hierarchy influence their kind and decisions."

"This is finally a topic I can agree with." The girl who tried to trip me smiled and leaned back in her seat, crossing her legs.

"I'm sure you do." Professor Shaw laughed and pointed the pen at her. "So, start us off. What's your belief?"

"That blood and power are everything." She glanced at me and smirked. "And we take care of our own."

"Yes, blood and power are almost interchangeable." He wrote the words blood and power on the board before turning back around. "For vampires, this is both their weakness and strength. At times, their thirst for the blood of someone can become an obsession. Something they can't quite control."

"Hey now." The girl pouted and crossed her arms.

"Oh, come on now. That's been proven over and over throughout history." He paced in front of the room. "For example, the legend of Count Dracula. He came to an end because of his cravings and urges. However, real vampires can reproduce and rarely turn someone into one of them. They can control their venom. The only thing the legend had right was that their heart doesn't beat, which makes them immortal."

Wow, this guy was super passionate about these facts. Maybe this wouldn't be such a bad class after all.

"All right." He glanced at the clock and smiled. "Sorry for holding you over, but this is exciting information."

The class had been truly interesting and insightful. It

was amazing how the teacher was able to break down the core characteristics of each supernatural race.

Everyone grabbed their stuff and headed out of the room without even a backward glance. However, the vampire girl hissed at me before disappearing.

"So, what did you think of the class?" Professor Shaw erased the board and dusted off his hands.

"It was truly interesting." I stood from my desk and stretched out my back.

"I'm glad. Students either love the class or hate it." He shrugged and turned around.

"Well, it is a little concerning knowing everyone is learning about your strengths and weaknesses. Sometimes those secrets are best kept hidden though." I understood why this information was needed, but it could help others get a strategic advantage over your kind.

"Any good leader already knows this information whether through this class or learning on their own." He adjusted his shirt and smiled. "It's what this university is supposed to do. Generate the future leaders of our races."

"I think each of us will learn a lot." A whiff of cotton candy floated into the room.

"Hey, teach. How's our girl doing?" Cole swaggered in and wrapped an arm around my shoulders.

"Your girl?" The professor had a strange look on his face as he pulled back, taking in what was happening right in front of him.

"Yup, I was the recruit who brought her in." He tugged me further into his side. "So I guess I'm responsible for her now."

"You do realize that you've recruited several hundred others for us." The professor waved his hands side to side. "And you've never done this before."

"Don't be jealous." He placed a hand on his chest. "I still have room here for you too."

It was official. Cole had no boundaries at all.

"Aw. Thank you, Mr. Smith." He rubbed a hand down his face. "You've eased all my concerns. Now, Miss Wright, if you need any help getting caught up, please let me know. We hadn't really gotten into any of the details prior to today. It was more about why you needed this information and what to do with it. So, please, come to me if needed. I have an open-door policy."

"Now, don't be trying to steal her from me." Cole dropped his hand from my shoulders and gently grabbed my arm. "If she needs any extra help, I'm more than willing to give it to her ... if you know what I mean."

Oh my God. I may have died of embarrassment right then if I hadn't already. "I have a boyfriend, and it's not him."

"That's good to know." He tsked and pointed his finger at Cole. "You're making her uncomfortable, and I don't blame her either. Rest assured Ms. Wright; I already know that Mr. Smith is quite full of it, so don't worry."

"Aw, Ravey's face is red." Cole tapped me on my nose. "Somehow that makes you even more adorable. This may have to become a regular occurrence."

"Please, don't." I'm pretty sure he would try to top himself next time, and there was no telling how far he would go. "I'm not sure I could survive it."

"I think it's time both of you go and grab some dinner." The professor glanced at me and motioned Cole to the door. "I would tell you to stop embarrassing her, Mr. Smith, but I think that might only encourage you more."

"Challenge accepted." He lifted both hands and pretended to shoot Professor Shaw.

"He didn't even challenge you." That was the point of the professor's whole spiel.

"Oh, he did." Cole tugged me to the door. "It's the fact that he didn't challenge me that made it a challenge."

"Do you even listen to yourself sometimes?" Cole must live in a different world than the rest of us. That was the only answer.

"Sweet Miss Wright, I think the problem is that he listens to himself way more than he should." The professor shrugged and once again glanced at my necklace.

At least I'm hoping that he was eyeing my necklace and not my boobs. That would be even more disconcerting.

Cole dragged me out of the classroom and into the hall. "How did your first day with Professor Shaw go?"

"It was really interesting." For once, I didn't have to lie about a class. "I knew the basics about the other supernaturals, but we weren't around them. Somehow we had isolated ourselves. Still, learning more about all the strengths and weaknesses, it's interesting. Although it's also …"

"Unnerving?" Cole guided me through the crowded halls, ignoring all the people who stared at me.

"Yes, that's the word I was looking for." It was surprising that he got it. He was always cutting jokes, so I wasn't entirely sure he'd understand.

He opened a glass door that led outside, and when we stepped through, his shoulders sagged. "There is good in that class, but it's still relatively new." He ran his hands through his hair, causing the spikes to be messy. "It's something the Professor had been trying for years to push through, and the headmaster finally approved it just this past semester."

"Really?" At least this confirmed what I had initially thought. It was one thing to know about the other races, but to lay out each strength and weakness in front of everyone didn't completely sit well with me. However, if we were the next set of leaders coming through, it would be good to know just for the sake of interaction and respect.

"There is a benefit to knowing, but having each race dissected like that may not be the best idea." He glanced off into the woods and frowned. "This is his pilot class that you're in."

"Thanks for telling me." Now my concerns were amplified. Cole must have been more concerned than I was, considering the way he was acting. All traces of the strong, inappropriate vampire I'd come to know were gone.

"Still, for it to bother you as a newbie, it proves my concerns aren't one-sided." A door opened and shut, and footsteps headed in our direction. Cole's eyes narrowed, and he stood close to me.

Great. Jordan's dark hair almost blended into the black tight shirt she wore, and her lips were painted a blood red. "Am I interrupting something?"

"No, not at all." Cole reached out his arm behind me, propping himself up on a tree. "We were discussing bitches, so it must have summoned one. I'm not surprised it was you who got the call."

She stopped and balled her hands at her sides. "What did I ever do to you?"

"Breathe." His tone grew colder somehow. "You're wasting a precious commodity."

Before I could help it, a giggle escaped me.

"Aw, your little pet thinks it okay for her to make a noise." She opened her mouth, and her fangs extended. "Maybe I should teach her a lesson. After all, dogs were made to die."

"Watch it, Jordan." Cole smirked and leaned closer to me. "Your jealousy is beginning to show."

"Once upon a time, I might have thought you were the best catch around." She crossed her arms right under her breasts, emphasizing them. "But not anymore. How could you befriend someone like her?"

"Because unlike you, he knows that I'm only a bitch to those who are deserving." I'd never disliked someone as much as her. I thought I hated Sheila before, but at that moment, I could see that Sheila wasn't even close to being an eighth annoying as Jordan was.

Jordan cringed at my words, and her body stiffened. "Did I give you permission to speak to me?"

"Count yourself lucky that the two of us are giving you the time of day." Cole glanced toward the woods and smiled. "Maybe that's the lesson you need. You get your thrills from feeling in charge. What would happen if no one talked to you?"

"You aren't God, Cole." She lifted her chin, but there was fear in her eyes. "There is no way you could make that happen."

"That's bullshit, and you know it." Cole stood straight and advanced on her. Each step toward her, she backed up another step. "You mess with Raven one more time, and I'll make that happen. Is that what you want?"

Her bottom lip quivered, and her eyes landed on me with even more hatred than before. "You better watch your back." She turned around and hurried back into the building, slamming the door behind her.

Damien's pine smell hit my nose.

"Did you really have to do that?" Damien stepped from the woods and shook his head.

"Please tell him that she approached us." Cole stuck his hands into the pockets of his jeans.

"He's telling the truth." I had to protect Cole. He'd done it enough for me. "She wanted the altercation."

"She won't let it go." A side of Damien's lips lifted. "She's like a dog with a bone."

"What? Did you just compare her to a dog?" Cole glanced around and pouted. "Damnit, there was no one here to witness that."

"That's enough, Cole." Damien frowned and rubbed his eyes. "The more you keep antagonizing, the more people are going to go after her."

I couldn't believe that Damien was worried about my well-being. He was so quiet and standoffish.

"Aw, you care for her too." Cole arched an eyebrow.

"No, but for some reason, I've teamed up with you and Rage." Damien stepped toward me and seemed to be examining me. "I'm not sure why, but you both care about her. So, if you really care, stop antagonizing people."

If that didn't make it clear how he felt about me, I wasn't sure what else would. I was obviously a nuisance, and he was doing this just for his friends. Still, Damien was right. For whatever reason, Cole was determined we'd be friends. So how exactly was I going to fit in here?

CHAPTER TWELVE

The last six months had been crazy, to say the least. Luckily, we got into a pattern. Rage still avoided me like the plague, and Cole put some distance between us, at least from what everyone else saw. Of course, Greg called and texted me every day.

Jordan and her crew seemed to settle down when Cole stopped publicly hanging around me. All of them still hated me, but her blatant attempts to make my life hell had reduced drastically.

My biggest concern was that I still wasn't able to fully connect with my wolf. Damien was getting frustrated with me, and to be honest, so was I. It was like there was some kind of barrier. Damien had told Cole to stop hanging around because I had no way to protect myself yet.

Christmas was already upon us. Still, I wasn't allowed to go home because of my issues. After what I had done to Damien, they were afraid that it could happen again. For some reason, Damien wanted to stay here and help me gain control. The break gave us another two weeks of training with no interference from anyone else.

Everyone was getting ready to head home, but there was a dance tonight for the students and staff.

Something was being dragged across the den floor, and I jumped out of bed to see what was going on. When I entered the den, I found Jess with an oversized suitcase with clothes sticking out the sides. She was attempting to tug it to the door, but the suitcase probably weighed more than she did.

"Do you need some help?" I couldn't help the grin that spread across my face.

"Hmmph, no." She tugged on it once more, but it didn't even budge an inch. "Fine, but I don't want any gloating to happen."

"No promises." I couldn't help digging at her. She normally never needed help so this was a rare opportunity.

"Hey now." When she saw the look on my face, she sighed. "Girl, don't play me like that."

"You know I love you too much to follow through." I walked over and grabbed the luggage. It was even hard for me to carry. "What the hell do you have in here?"

"Well, my clothes here are nicer than the ones at home." She cringed and shrugged. "So maybe ... uh, over half my closet."

"How did they all fit in here?" Our closets were pretty full, and most of them were our standard button-down shirts and skirts.

"I might've used some of my magic." She shrugged. "It's no big deal."

"Are you leaving already?" My stomach dropped. I'd assumed she and I would go to the dance together.

"Of course not." She reached over and swatted my arm. "I just know it'll be hard for me to get out of bed in the morning. My parents are coming bright and early to take me back home."

"Your parents are coming?" She hadn't told me that little nugget of information before now.

"Yeah, didn't I tell you?" She tapped her finger to her lips. "Oh, wait. I was going to, and then Damien pulled you away for training. Oops." She cringed and then smiled at me. "Hey Raven, my parents want to meet you so they are picking me up."

"Thanks for the heads up." It wasn't a big deal at all, but I had to tease her a little more. "So, I guess I shouldn't go to bed naked tonight."

"If you want to make a lasting impression, sure." She shrugged and fell back onto the couch. "I won't judge."

"There goes my confidence in you telling me if something is a bad idea." It was crazy how close we'd become in this short amount of time. I figured living with someone inadvertently did that.

"Speaking of which, we need to go dress shopping." She crossed her legs and picked at her nails. "We should've already done this."

"How are we going to get off campus?" Neither one of us had a car, so I'd planned on rolling in with just jeans and a shirt.

"Did you really just ask me that?" She jumped to her feet and hurried down the hallway to my room.

"What are you doing?" If she was hoping for some cute dresses in there, she was going to be sadly mistaken.

She walked into my room and was back out within seconds with my cell phone in her hands. "I'm taking this emergency into my own hands." She swiped my phone, entering the correct design to gain access to contacts.

"How do you know my password?" I'd never given it to her before.

"Oh, come on." She rolled her eyes as she operated my phone. "It's a freaking square. Do you know how boring that is?"

"No, but I'm pretty sure you just told me." That had me worried about how many others knew it. I was going to have to change it before she did some kind of spell on it where it couldn't be changed.

"That's what friends do." She typed something into the phone and then tossed it to me. "There, problem solved."

I glanced at the phone and saw what she'd texted.

Hey Cole - I need a trip to town.

"Really?" I was never going to hear the end of it.

"Oh, come on." She placed her hand on her hip. "You love him."

"He's like a fungus." The more I asked him for stuff, the more I knew I'd never live it down. "He takes hold and won't leave."

"I'm so telling him you said that." Jess laughed and moved past me.

The phone buzzed in my hand.

Ohhh! Are we buying lingerie? I'd be more than happy to let you know which outfit works best. Meet me at my car in ten.

Of course, that would be his response. "We've got to meet him in ten. You better get ready." I slammed my door and rushed, throwing on a pair of jeans and a t-shirt. Even though it was late December, it wasn't super cold here, so my wolf alone kept me warm.

I raced into the bathroom and grabbed the toothbrush rather than my hairbrush. I quickly applied some lip stain and mascara. Thankfully, it didn't take me long, I headed into the den.

"What took you so long?" Jess was pacing back and forth. "I was ready to go before."

"Girl, it's only been like five minutes." I wasn't sure if I was up to handling both her and Cole this morning. Hell, I hadn't even had a cup of coffee yet. I slipped on my tennis shoes and grabbed my purse. "Let's go."

"It's about damn time." Jess swung open the door and rushed to the elevator.

I wasn't sure what the hell I was getting into. I glanced at my phone again and cringed. It had just turned nine, and they were already dragging me to go shopping.

Within minutes, we were out the door and heading to the parking lot. Since it was a Saturday morning and right before the dance, we had been blessed to have a day off to rest and relax. Obviously, I wouldn't be partaking in any of that.

"Damn, do you know which car is his?" Jess glanced around the rather small parking lot.

Cole appeared in front of us and waved us toward him.

"How the hell did he get here so fast?" He was nowhere in sight, and then within a blink of an eye, he stood right in front of us.

"He's a vampire." She didn't even bother glancing in my direction. She was on a mission. "That's one of their things."

Of course I knew that, but Cole had never used that skill on me.

As we approached him, his blue eyes seemed to sparkle in the sun. "So, I'm thinking we'd start with Victoria's Secret. I mean, yes, it's like the staple guy thing to say, but I'm open to other places after we leave there."

"When did Victoria's Secret begin selling dresses?" Jess paused and grabbed her phone.

"Dresses. Okay." He nodded and glanced off into the distance. "Sure, that would be classier, but you'd need a lot of lace or leather."

"Leather does sound sexy." She nodded as she kept swiping on her phone.

"We aren't going to Victoria's Secret." I needed a damn cup of coffee and pronto. "First we're going to Starbucks and then to a store that sells dresses. Apparently, I need a dress for the shindig tonight."

"Shindig?" Jess stopped paying attention to her phone and looked at me. "What's that?"

"But you'd still need new underwear for underneath." Cole nodded at me with a very serious expression on his face.

"The shindig of which she speaks is the dance." Rage walked up to us from behind. "And no, no new underwear." His earthy scent hit me a little too late since he'd already made his presence known.

"Oh, come on." Cole pouted and raised both hands. "Every girl has to have new underwear for a dance."

"Who the hell told you that?" Sometimes I worried about him and his ideas.

"Common knowledge." Cole huffed and pulled out his keys.

"No, this girl right here is fine with her underwear. I just need a dress." There was no way I'd be modeling anything ever for Cole.

"New underwear wouldn't hurt though." Jess smashed her lips together, trying to keep from grinning.

"No." It had been a nice friendship while it lasted. "It's not happening. Or if it does, that's just between you and

Cole." At this point, I was wanting to march back into the dorm and crawl back into bed. I wasn't sure I could take a full day with these two ding-a-lings. "Please, for the love of God, I need coffee, stat."

Rage grabbed the keys from Cole's hands and headed to the car. "Now that's the best idea I've heard in the last five minutes." He hurried over, opened the front passenger door, and held it open. "Let's get moving. If those two want to join, they'll jump in."

This was the closest I'd been to him for a while, and his scent made my head a little dizzy. "Thanks." I wasn't sure how the word got out of my mouth, but it did even if it was a little breathy.

I slid into the seat, and he shut the door. He didn't skip a beat as he walked past Cole and Jess.

"Hey, what are you doing?" Cole followed behind, but it was too late. Rage had already opened the driver door, got behind the wheel, and even locked his door behind himself.

"Dude, this is my car." Cole reached to open the door, but it wouldn't budge.

"If you want to go, get in the back seat." Rage motioned behind him.

"Hell, no. This is my fucking car." He narrowed his eyes and extended his fangs.

"What the hell?" Every nerve in my body was on end.

"Don't worry." Rage whispered as he grabbed the gear stick and put it in reverse. "He'll get in and get over it fast too."

"So you've done this before?" It surprised me that this might be a common occurrence.

"Nope, but I was trying to make you feel better." He grinned at me, and my body reacted inappropriately.

The door behind me opened, and Jess climbed in. "You guys aren't going anywhere, not without me."

"I sure hope so since you were the one who got me up this damn early." I could've been in bed sleeping, but Jess had ruined that.

Cole jerked the back driver's side door open and got in. "Not cool."

"Sorry, man, but if you drove, we'd be heading straight to Victoria's Secret or some other specialty store. I don't think I could handle that today." Rage turned on the A/C, blasting it.

Those words and the A/C were like a cold shower to me. I didn't know why, but I thought he might be having a hard time fighting his feelings for me just like I was for him. Still, if both of us fighting our attraction didn't make it clear, I wasn't sure what else could.

"Well, you could be right." Cole leaned forward and winked at me. "I mean, hot girls with barely anything on. If that's not a good start to the day, I'm not sure what else would be."

"Can you please just drop this?" If I had to hear the words underwear one more time, I might have spontaneously combusted.

We hit the main road heading into town. Everyone in the car was in complete silence until my eyes landed on the Starbucks logo, and I groaned. "Thank God."

Cole cleared his throat. "Whatcha doin' up there, Ravey? Do we need a hand check?" He leaned between the seats, scanning me over.

"What the hell are you doing?" I reached over and smacked him on top of the head.

"It just sounded like you might be pleas ..."

"Shut the hell up, Cole." Rage clutched his fingers on

the steering wheel and shook his head. "She just saw a Starbucks."

"I'm just saying, this has been probably the best morning of my entire life." Jess giggled in the backseat.

When Rage pulled into the parking lot, I got out and stretched my legs. Cole was a handful, so I probably needed a double shot of something in order to get through the day.

Jess and Cole headed straight into Starbucks, but I needed a moment to myself.

"What's your usual?" Rage stepped up to me and scanned me over.

He always gave me mixed signals. One second, I'd think he was attracted to me, and in the next, he didn't seem interested at all. It shouldn't matter. After all, I still had Greg, but a part of me knew that relationship wouldn't amount to anything. "A venti non-fat blonde vanilla latte."

His indifferent face morphed into one of pure confusion. "Okay, wasn't expecting that at all. I was expecting mocha or regular coffee. Not whatever it is you just said."

"Hey, don't shade me." I stuck my tongue out at him. "I just know what I like."

"I wished that was true." The words were so low I thought I'd dreamed them. He nodded to the door. "You ready?"

"Go on without me." At least he seemed to not hate my guts. "I need another moment of peace before I head into that."

"Yeah, he's a handful." A genuine smile crossed his face. "At least Jess seems to hold her own."

Damn, I was in trouble. That unguarded smile might have been my undoing. "That she can." Thankfully some coherent words made it through, so I wasn't just awkwardly gawking at him.

"Alright, let me go brave the vampire." He winked at me and walked across the parking lot.

I was completely at his mercy as I watched his ass the entire way to the building. Damn, I had to get myself together. My phone dinged, alerting me to a text message. When I saw Greg's name, I felt really guilty even though I hadn't done anything.

Hey babe, I hope to see you soon. <3

It had been over six months since we last saw each other, and the way we had left things wasn't the best. At this point, I knew what I had to do, but damn, I wanted to do it in person. He at least deserved that, but not letting me go home over the holidays took me by surprise. However, Damien offered to stay back and work with me. He had said something about his parents doing Christmas overseas without him.

"You were the one hollering for coffee, and you're still standing out here?" Jess took a sip of her coffee and waited for me by the door. "Get your ass in here already. We have to make sure we have ample time for dress shopping."

My chance at killing some time had just ended. "They don't open until ten. We still have," I said as I glanced at my watch, "thirty minutes."

"By the time you get in line and we get out of here, it'll be perfect timing." Her cheeks were flushed, and the wind blew her hair to the side.

"Alright, let's do this." I opened the door and went to join the line.

"Hey, come here." Rage motioned for me. "You don't need to stand in that line."

"Uh, yeah, I do." It was just like a man to forget who wanted to come here in the first place. "If you want to come out of this whole thing alive, I'd recommend you wait for me to get something."

"What if I want to be naughty?" Cole lifted the car keys and jiggled them.

Rage smacked Cole's hand, causing the keys to fall to the ground. "Just ignore him. I already ordered yours, so you're good to go."

My heart warmed at his words. What was going on with me? "Thanks, you didn't have to do that." The last time we'd talked, it had been right before Ashley went berserk in the cafeteria. It was tense, to say the least, so him being considerate was doing things to me that it really shouldn't have. He was a freaking player, so I had to keep my head on straight.

Jess nudged me in the side. "He got yours."

"You know he can hear you, right?" She's a supernatural and should know that shifters have amazing hearing.

"You know I don't care, right?" She elbowed me again and snickered. "Just sayin' he didn't get mine."

I gave her my best death glare, but she only dissolved into giggles.

"Blonde nonfat vanilla latte for Raven." The barista placed the drink on the table and went back to work.

"What the hell is that?" Cole advanced slowly toward the cup. "When you ordered it, I thought you were talking about Jess."

"Why in the hell would I be ordering for Jess?" Rage rubbed a hand down his face. "You know what. I don't want to know. Forget I asked."

"I'm glad you asked the question." Cole pointed at Rage and then rubbed his chin. "Because I thought that was a more plausible explanation instead of it being a fucking frou-frou coffee drink."

A few younger girls sitting at a table nearby giggled, checking both of the guys out. My wolf wanted to come unhinged.

"First off, thank you." I grabbed my drink from the table and headed to the door. "Now, let's go. We've already been everyone's daily entertainment."

Jess followed right on my heels, and when we stepped outside, she touched my arm. "Girl, I'm only having fun, but you need to be careful with Rage. Granted, he never treated Ashley like this. Still, don't give away your milk for free. Make him buy the whole damn cow."

If this was any indication of how my day would keep going, I definitely needed to go back to my room and crawl into bed. I had a vampire that was inappropriate as hell, a player that was making my insides turn to mush, and a fae giving me dairy quotes about sex. I hoped there was only one way up from here.

CHAPTER THIRTEEN

My only salvation was my bougie coffee drink that everyone made fun of. I blocked out all the ramblings as I sat behind Cole and next to Jess. I was relieved that I got a little bit of distance from Rage, but the way Cole was driving made me regret it. I think we ran at least three red lights and blew through two stop signs. I'd never been honked at this many times in my whole life. "I don't remember you driving like this before."

"Well, you were already going through a lot that day, so I behaved." Cole glanced at me through the rearview mirror. "Thank God I don't have to anymore."

"I've never ridden with you before, so you could behave for me." Jess clutched onto the door handle for dear life.

"You can't complain." She was the one who had texted Cole, not me. "This is all your doing."

"Just pull over. I'll run the rest of the way." Rage turned around and glanced at me.

"You can't do that." Cole let go of the steering wheel and surveyed the area. "We're in a freaking town. Someone would see you shift, and then shit would hit the fan."

Luckily, the storefront came into view, so we had to survive only a few more seconds of misery.

"See, here we are." Cole squealed his tires as he flew into the parking lot and drove at least fifty miles per hour to the front parking space. There was no one even attempting to get it, but he didn't slow down until he skidded into the parking space while slamming on his brakes.

Desperate to get out of the car, I yanked on the handle and tumbled out. Somehow, I was able to save my latte.

"Now don't be dramatic." Cole frowned and slammed his door shut. "It wasn't that bad."

"Speak for yourself." Jess held her stomach, and her face was a little pale. "I may puke."

"That's it." Rage shook his head and grabbed the keys from Cole. "I'm driving us back. End of discussion."

"I'm feeling a little ganged up on right now." Cole pouted and glanced at the ground. "I don't like it."

Now, I kind of felt bad. "It wasn't that horrible; it was just a little rough. Oh, and a couple of things were unexpected."

"Yeah, like when the bus was in the intersection and you ran a red light." Jess grabbed my arms and placed some of her weight on me. "All I had seen was the bus coming right at my door, and I swear I could hear the driver screaming as he narrowly missed us."

"Or when the old people rode their bicycles in the bicycle zone, and you decided that you could go faster in that lane instead of the main road." I still cringed at the memory. "The old man had to fall on the ground to escape you clipping his bike."

"He stood back up, though." Cole threw his hands to the side. "So, he couldn't be injured that badly."

Jess grabbed her phone and smiled. "Alright, it's ten.

Let's get shopping." She marched right to the doors as if she was daring them to still be locked.

"Why are we here?" Rage walked beside me, taking his time. "I'm assuming the lingerie talk was something Cole was hoping for and not actually happening."

"You'd be correct on that." I took the last sip of my drink and threw the cup into one of the garbage cans in front of the strip mall. "I'm getting a dress for tonight."

"Oh, you're going?" He focused hard on the doors in front of us.

"With Jess, I doubt I have an option." Besides, all my other high school dances had been with Greg. We'd always end up eating with his crew. After it was over, we'd wind up at one of his friend's parties, which involved him getting plastered and trying to feel me up. I'd finish the night by dragging him home and letting him sleep it off. This was a chance for me to do it my way.

"So, who are you going with?" He cleared his throat and looked away from me.

Was he fishing for information? Let's have a little fun. "Well, they are hot and fun to be with."

There was a tick in his neck, and his jaw tightened. "I hadn't realized you made that many friends here."

"I'm going with Jess." He thought I was dating someone at school. "And she has to make sure we look perfect, so here we are."

We were silent as we entered Macy's together. Cole passed us by and headed over to the guy's section. "Don't worry, man. I'm going to find something that will make us look good too."

"Oh, dear God." Rage sighed and shook his head. "I better go with him. Otherwise, he'll have me wearing a pink tux or something worse."

"Girl, come on." Jess hollered at me and appeared from behind a rack of clothes. "We've got to hurry. We still have to get ready."

"Duty calls." I hated that this moment with Rage was ending, but at the same time, it needed to. I couldn't get attached for several reasons, and the main one was Greg. Even though I realized we didn't work, he deserved more than a text or a phone call to end it. We had spent over two and a half years together. Granted, the last six months had me here while he was there. Secondly, even if Greg and I were broken up, Rage wasn't the one I'd need to fall for. It would just leave my heart shattered.

"Have fun." He winked at me, and my knees became wobbly.

Not wanting to become an awkward gawker, I forced myself to join Jess. "So, what are we shopping for? I haven't been to a dance here before."

"Girl, think prom." Jess pulled out a red feathered lacy dress that was low cut and tight. It flattered her pale skin and blonde hair. The feathers seemed to move when she took a step while just holding it, totally embodying the fae look.

"Try that one on." If she didn't, I would, and it wouldn't look quite as great on me.

"That's what I was thinking." She flipped through a few more dresses and pulled out a shimmery green dress that had a slit from the upper thigh all the way to the floor. "Ooh, and this one."

She hurried off to the fitting room as I stayed back, flipping through the rack. There were all sorts of pretty dresses, but I was low on funds. Unlike most of the kids attending Bloodshed, my parents didn't have a ton of money. From what I gathered, even Jess was from a wealthy family, just not filthy rich and one of 'the' families that usually got in—kinda like me, except for the cash.

My phone vibrated again, but I didn't even bother looking at it. Greg had been texting a lot here lately. It was as if he felt our impending doom as well.

"How does it look?" Jess stepped out wearing the red dress and twirled.

"It looks great." I almost believed that if she wore a potato sack, she'd still look amazing.

"Yeah?" She spun around and sighed. "It's so tight around my thighs though. I'm afraid it'll make it hard to dance."

"Well, then. Try on the other one." I turned back to the racks and found a black strapless dress that was gorgeous. I glanced at the price tag and cringed. It wasn't as bad as I was expecting, but still, I couldn't afford it.

"Ohhh, that's gorgeous." Jess rushed back out with the shimmery green dress on. "You should try it on."

"I don't think I'll get anything." I didn't want to tap into my parents' funds more than I already had. "That dress is amazing. I think it's the one."

"Yes, I do too." She twirled around, and the dress bounced. "And it'll be great for dancing too." She reached over and grabbed the hanger of the dress I'd just been eyeing. "Go put this on, and let's look at it."

"No, seriously I'm fine." I wished I hadn't agreed to come here. I blamed it on my lack of caffeine.

"If you go try it on, I promise not to give you any more grief." Jess laid her hand on her heart.

"Fine." I wanted to try it on. Here's hoping I looked horrible in it.

"You're not heading toward a death sentence. Try to

smile." Jess giggled and wrapped an arm around me. "You're only trying on a dress."

She was right, but I refused to tell her that. "Let's get this over with."

Jess entered her dressing room and started changing back into her clothes.

I entered the room right next to her and quickly undressed. This dress just has to look horrible on me. I repeated it several times, hoping the words would make it come true. I slipped the dress on and zipped up the back. When I turned to the mirror, I paused.

Not only did the strapless dress look great on me, it somehow enhanced my breasts. An intricate design of cubic zirconia stones wrapped around my waist, and the dress stopped right above my knees with several layers of thin black material over the base. Damn, it was gorgeous.

"Let me see." Jess demanded from outside my changing room.

The last thing I wanted to do was open the door. Knowing her though, she'd climb through the opening at the bottom. I opened the door, and Jess's mouth dropped open. "Oh my God. You rock that dress."

Yes, I did. It didn't matter since it was too expensive. "Nah, I'm sure I can find something just as nice back home." I closed the door and changed back into my clothes. As I hung the dress back on the hanger, I allowed myself to pout for all of one second.

I opened the door to find Jess waiting for me at the entrance. "All right. Let's get going."

"You're going to look amazing tonight." I was happy for her.

"Do you know where the guys went?" Jess glanced both directions.

"They are in the men's area." Or at least that's what Cole had said earlier.

"Well, we've been here for an hour. I'm hungry and in need of getting back. We have to get ready." She glanced at her phone and frowned. "Do you mind finding them while I check out?"

"Don't mind at all." I turned to go put my dress back when Jess grabbed my arm.

"I'll put it back on my way to the register." She pointed to the customer service desk to the left. "Go ahead and find them. There's no telling what Cole is up to."

Now that was a fair statement. The one thing you could count on was Cole being unpredictable. It was like he fed off of it. "All right, I'll meet ya up front." I headed to the right, looking for the men's area.

"See, if you wore this, we'd be the talk of the night." Cole's voice came from the discount section.

I found Cole decked out in a black suit that had red hearts all over the jacket, pants, and even the tie.

He was holding up a similar suit to his, but instead of hearts, it had dollar signs. "You could be R Money and I could be C Lover."

"C Lover? Really?" Rage sat in a chair, leaned over with his head in his hands. "Do you know what that could mean?"

"Candy lover? Cat lover?" Cole stared at the ceiling and tapped his lips. "Cook lover?"

"Sometimes I wonder how we're even friends." Rage sniffed and glanced in my direction. "Tell him to stop ... please."

"I'm with Rage on this one." They would definitely be the talk of the school. "Do you really want your elitist and elusive persona tarnished by this? People might think you're funny and awkward."

"Dammit." Cole frowned and glanced in the mirror. "You're right. We can't have that." He turned and headed back to the men's dressing area.

"Wait." Rage sat straight and blinked several times. "Did you just reason with Cole?"

"It's actually quite simple if you know how." When it came to his reputation, he cared way too much. The only thing that helped him maintain it was the fact that he didn't let many people in.

"Thank you." Rage sighed and chuckled. "I was honestly afraid he'd demand I wear that shit."

"Hey, that's what friends are for." The words slipped out before I could take them back. I didn't want to just be his friend, and even worse, I implied that I considered him one.

"Did you just friend zone me?" His mouth dropped open, and he flinched.

There was no way to salvage this. Either way I went, it would have come out wrong. "I'm not sure what we are."

"But you do feel something?" He reached out and touched my hand. His face was filled with something similar to hope.

"Yes, but there is Greg." This was a dangerous game I was playing, but I felt like I needed to tell him the truth. "I haven't broken up with him yet."

"Yet. That means you're going to?" There was something sort of desperate in his words.

"Fine, you both win." Cole walked out from the fitting room and frowned. "You guys will just have to deal with my fine ass in a black suit."

"Your timing is impeccable today." Rage stood and growled. "Let's get out of here."

"Don't worry though." Cole moved beside me as I followed Rage. "We'll still have fun."

"I wasn't ever worried about it not being fun." I rubbed my arms, trying to make the moments before disappear. At the end of the day, I couldn't lose my focus on what truly mattered.

"It's about time you guys showed up." Jess had her dress covered with plastic. "I'm ready to get back."

"What? That's it?" Cole's forehead wrinkled, and he took a step back.

"We have to get ready. No spoilers." Jess rolled her eyes and waved a hand along her body. "Beauty takes time. After all, the dance starts at six."

"Don't worry." Rage lifted his closed hand with his palm facing downward and then flicked his fingers open. The keys hung on his middle finger. "I've got the keys, so no more near-death experiences."

At least there was one miracle for the day. "I can say that I'm not upset about that."

"All this shade is making me chilly." Cole shivered as if he was cold. "For this, a harsh punishment will be dealt." He winked at me. "Next time you need a ride, someone will be modeling at least one pair of underwear for me."

"That sounds fair." I already knew what we could do.

"What?" He startled and put his hand to his ear. "Did I just hear someone agree?" An evil grin crossed his face. "Hell, yeah."

"Let's go before he begins demanding other things." Rage's eyes landed on me for a moment, causing my heart to speed up. He grinned.

As we arrived back at the academy, Jess was about to bubble over. "Tonight is going to be so much fun."

"Why do girls get excited about all these things?" Cole frowned. "All we do is dress uncomfortably."

"We also get to look our best." Jess lifted her dress in the air as the wind blew the plastic.

"Hey, why are there two dresses?" That little sneak. She bought my dress too.

"Probably because she was afraid she'd change her mind, so she bought a back-up." Cole grinned as if he discovered the meaning of life.

"No, she bought the dress I liked too." I headed over to her and went for the bottom of the plastic cover.

"There is only one dress." Her face turned pink, and she nodded her head repeatedly. "Maybe the green just looked dark for a second."

"Uh ... no." Rage appeared behind her and grabbed her shoulders. "It did not."

Now that he was holding her in place, I raised the plastic. Sure enough, there was her dress and mine. "Jess ..."

"Look, I wanted to do it, okay?" Jess shot Rage a dirty look and faced me. "Last year, I didn't go because I didn't have a friend. And this time, I do. I wanted to get it so we both could have fun getting dressed together and because you looked damn hot in it."

I hated the fact that she bought it, but she was more excited about it than I was. "Thank you. I really appreciate it."

"You're welcome." Her eyes glowed, and she pulled the plastic back in place. "We don't want them getting messed up."

As we headed off to our dorm room, Rage reached out and grabbed my arm. "Hey, do you have a second?"

Jess giggled and stayed put.

"Yeah, sure." He led me several yards away from the others before he stopped. "So ... I know you still have that loser, but maybe you could save a dance or two for me?"

My wolf howled through me, but I forced her back in place. "Maybe." I didn't want to commit to something. Not while I was still technically with Greg.

"I'll take that." Rage grinned and moved closer to me. His earthy scent surrounded me, and for the first time in a while, I relaxed.

"Raven?" An all too familiar voice called out to me.

No, it couldn't be. It had to be my guilt messing around with me. I turned, and there, not even fifty feet away, was my boyfriend. "Greg?"

"Well, I came here to surprise you, but it looks like I got one instead." His eyes flashed back and forth between Rage and me.

"So, you're saying she can't have guy friends?" Cole jumped into action. He closed the distance between us and wrapped an arm around my waist. "I thought you were an alpha. Instead, someone sounds really insecure."

Pure hate flashed in Greg's eyes. It brought me right back to graduation when he discovered I was the one they wanted—not him. "Why don't you mind your own business?"

"Hi, Greg." Jess stepped forward in front of us and held her hand out. "Raven has said a lot of nice things about you. It's great to finally meet you."

Thank goodness, at least one of them was trying to help defuse the situation.

"I'm surprised she found time." He crossed his arms and leaned back.

"What are you doing here?" I created some distance between me and the guys to hopefully alleviate some of the tension.

He sighed. "Your parents told my Dad that you wouldn't make it home this Christmas and that there was a dance tonight. So I thought I'd come down here and take you to the dance."

A deep growl filled the air. Rage was breathing rapidly, and the air grew tense.

Both Rage and Greg were on the edge. Each alpha ready to fight the other for dominance. I had to talk to Greg and let him know where we stood with each other. I always knew it wasn't going to be an easy conversation, but I didn't expect to have it here at Bloodshed Academy during a surprise visit. I only hoped that he'd keep his head on straight.

CHAPTER FOURTEEN

"What the hell is wrong with him?" Jess stood in her bathroom, organizing all her makeup. "He can't just show up here and pee on you."

Despite everything, that made me giggle. "He's always been like that." However, seeing it now with a new perspective, I guess Greg wasn't really as strong as he thought.

"Seriously, you dated him for two years?" She picked up something that looked like eyeliner and threw it into the garbage. "Maybe I should be asking what's wrong with you."

That was a fair statement. "You've got to realize I was raised with the mentality that no female could ever be a true alpha."

"Are you kidding me right now?" Jess paused with her organizing and turned toward me. Her eyes were wide, and her brows furrowed. "What backwoods hick town did you grow up in?"

"We were right outside Nashville." I always wondered why my parents moved there. They weren't from there and had grown up near New Orleans. "We didn't travel, just stayed put."

"Yeah, I've heard that there are hundreds of packs and supernatural societies that are still following old, outdated practices." She patted her bed and smiled. "Good thing Isadora can find the ones that deserve this chance. Now come on, let's get moving."

Suddenly there was a loud knock on her door. "Raven, I'm hungry. Let's go grab some food."

"She's busy," Jess yelled and marched over to the door, yanking it open.

Greg took a step back, surprise written all over his face. "I wasn't asking you."

Oh, dear God. This was not going to end well. "We're getting ready for the dance tonight. It starts in two hours." Needless to say, the past couple of hours with Greg here had been tense. We'd sat and watched a few shows, not knowing what to say to one another.

"Alright, I guess I'll go mosey around campus for a little while. Then come back and get ready." He turned away, and within a few seconds, the main door shut.

"At least he's gone." Jess spun around and snorted. "I have no idea what you ever saw in him." She grabbed a button-down shirt from her dresser and threw it at me. "Put this on."

"Honestly, it's what my parents expected of me and what I thought was the right thing." Now that I've been here, I couldn't imagine that life anymore. "I never was in love with him. That's why I need to break it off." I slipped my shirt off and put the one she'd given me on.

"Please tell me you're doing it tonight." Jess grabbed a brush and powder from the bathroom and strolled toward me. "Because I really don't know if I could handle him staying here more than a day."

"You're leaving in the morning, and this is an all-girl dorm." I hadn't even considered this yet. "So, I'm not sure where he'll be sleeping."

She swiped the brush into the powder and attacked my face.

I leaned back, trying to dodge the assault. "You're like ten times paler than me. I can't use your foundation."

"This is fae powder." She brought the offending weapon to her side. "It blends into whatever your skin color is. A person with red skin uses the same powder as me. It's magic."

"There are companies here that claim that too." I had my doubts that it worked as well as getting one that was actually made to blend with your skin color.

"Silly, this is truly magic." She put her fingers in the powder, and it clung to her skin, sparkling. "Once it's on the brush, it's ready to do its job. Trust me."

"Fine, but if you make me look like a clown, I will seek revenge." I trusted her without a shadow of a doubt. She'd been a constant friend since the first day I got here.

"Shush, you." Once again, the brush swiped across my face so many times I lost count. "Almost done."

"I think you've covered each area at least fifty times." I was a bare essential type of girl when it came to makeup. I usually wore mascara and lip stain. That was it, nothing else needed.

"We have to make sure it's even all over your face; otherwise, you might get splotchy." She placed the brush on the bed and rushed back into the bathroom. "Alright, since you're wearing black, let's do smokey eyes." She grabbed some eyeshadows and smaller brushes before heading back over. That's when the real torture began.

"See, voila." Jess stepped back and waved me to the mirror on her dresser.

Great, I wasn't sure if I was going to like what I saw. When I saw my reflection in the mirror, I was stunned. My usual long, straight, chestnut hair had loose waves, and my brown eyes seemed so much lighter with the smoky eyeshadow framing them. My foundation was flawless, and there was only a hint of pink on both my lips and cheeks. I'd never looked this way before. "You are fucking amazing."

"I'm so glad you like it." She giggled and looked at me. "It's easy to do when you have a great canvas to work with."

All my life, I had never considered my looks as beautiful. My main priority was keeping tabs on my wolf. She was a little volatile at times and fought against my hold. Nothing there had changed yet, but at least I wasn't as worried about her coming out. They knew what my weaknesses were here, for better or worse. "Thank you." They were two very simple words, but at the moment, I couldn't think of anything more true.

She sniffled and blinked her eyes. "No, don't you dare." She fanned her face and bit her bottom lip. "I can't cry. My eyes can't be puffy tonight."

"We definitely can't have that." I glanced back at myself and smiled. Maybe tonight wouldn't be so bad after all.

"Okay, my turn." She went inside the bathroom and grabbed another damn brush.

How many of those things can one girl have? My phone buzzed. I grabbed it and saw a message from Damien.

Hey - Professor Shaw wants us to meet him in the woods behind the dorms. Be there in five.

My heart pounded in my chest. It didn't make sense. Why did Professor Shaw want to meet us?

OK- on my way.

"Hey, Damien and Professor Shaw want to meet me, so I'm going to head out for a minute." Thankfully, Greg was still out and about, so I didn't have to sneak out.

Jess stuck her head out of the bathroom and pointed a sharp eyeliner pencil at me. "If you mess up your hair and face, there will be *hell* to pay. Got it?"

Damn, she might be tiny, but she was scary sometimes. "I got it, ma'am." I understood her concern. Every time I came back from one of my sessions with Damien, I was a hot mess. Sweat poured from my every orifice, and my hair looked like I had stuck my finger in an electric socket.

In less than a minute, I was outside, heading to the area Damien had alluded to. Soon, I caught Damien's scent and hurried in his direction.

Apparently, I was the last to show. "Is everything okay?"

"Yeah, but Professor Shaw might have figured out the main reason for your issue." Damien's face was unreadable, but his right eye twitched now and then. I'd learned a while ago it was his tell when he got stressed.

"One of the things I've noticed, Ms. Wright, is that you always wear that necklace." His eyes went straight to the crescent moon that laid on my chest. "When you are working hard on your studies or stressed, you tend to play with it."

This wasn't brand new information. "Okay?"

"Mr. Weston, here," Professor Shaw placed his hand on Damien's shoulder, "informed me that you've had your particular separation ever since you were sixteen, which is when wolf shifters begin to grow strong. When did you receive that necklace?"

My breath caught. "My mother gave it to me when I turned sixteen."

"I hate to say this, but I'm wondering if it might be spelled." He held out one of his hands. "I did some research and found that a simple touch by a wizard could lift it."

"Are you sure?" That sounded way too easy. All he had to do was touch it, and I'd be whole.

"Yes, wizards are not a common supernatural found in this world." He glanced around the woods and grinned. "See, we aren't at our strongest on Earth. Fae lands are where we prefer to dwell. Although there are a handful that will visit from time to time and others like me who hold important jobs here."

I glanced at Damien. I wasn't sure what to do. Wizards weren't known for their pure intentions or helping others.

He nodded his head yes.

This was one of those times when I had to make a decision. Only, this one seemed so innocent. Trusting Damien and my gut, I removed my necklace. I could see Mom cursing at me in my head, but she'd never have to know. I dropped the necklace into his extended hand.

It felt as though everything was happening in slow motion. The necklace sparkled from the reflecting moonlight as it dropped into the wizard's hand. When it touched his skin, a loud roar echoed in my ear. The sound pierced deep inside of me, and I fell to my knees.

Flashbacks began to play in my head. The time when my wolf didn't like how Greg treated me, various times when I should've stood my ground, and lastly, the night I attacked Damien. I had charged him and sunk my teeth into his neck. I tore at it despite Cole and Rage's screams of protest. The bear was going to hurt me; that was his goal, and I had to stop him. Then, something hard slammed into me, and I blacked out.

My wolf then began to blend with me and take its rightful place inside. Now I understood what they meant by not synced. We weren't two beings in the same body; we were always meant to be one.

Damien was on his knees beside me. "Are you okay?"

I opened my eyes and smiled. I could feel the glow in them begin to subside. "I'm more than okay."

The professor's face was a shade paler as he stood above me, looking down. "I can't believe it. It's true."

"Thank you for helping me." I still didn't trust him, but maybe he deserved a break.

His shock morphed into a huge grin. "Of course. I can't wait to see what you'll become now."

Okay, that was strange. What did he mean?

"Come on, let's get you back to the dorm." Damien helped me stand and wrapped an arm around my waist. His hand was large and hot. It felt so damn good.

"You know I can walk?" I needed distance. It felt like I had become another person. My emotions and senses were heightened.

"She'll be fine in the next few minutes." Professor Shaw began strolling deeper into the woods. "They had been two beings, and now they are one. She's just getting acclimated. I'm going to keep this necklace to ensure there are no residual effects."

We walked in silence back in the direction of the dorms. That wasn't unusual for us. Damien wasn't a big talker, and we'd grown comfortable with one another.

As we approached my dorm, he gave me a smile. "You look beautiful tonight. I hope you have a great time."

"Are you not going?" Cole and Rage were going, so I figured he would as well.

"No, they aren't really my thing." He kicked at the ground and then chuckled. "Honestly, I'll probably wind up there because of Cole. Though I'll sneak out really early."

"I think it'll be fun. Maybe you need to loosen up and stick around?"

"Raven?" Greg's voice appeared from behind me.

"What are you doing out here?" It surprised me to see him come out from the deeper part of the woods. Professor Shaw should've passed him, and I couldn't imagine he'd be okay with a random person this close to the university.

"Oh, I was traipsing around the grounds." His eyes fell on Damien. "This is the second time today I find my girlfriend talking to another guy. However, this time it's in the woods. Maybe I should be the one asking why you're out here."

A growl escaped my lips. "Maybe you should be asking yourself why you're so insecure."

Damien took a step closer to me and glared at Greg.

"Don't get so high and mighty." Greg's breathing became ragged. He hated feeling like he was being talked down to. "When you come back, I'll be your alpha. Don't fucking forget that."

This was the problem with little man syndrome. "If that was the case, then why am I the one here?"

A deep chuckle escaped Damien, and something that looked a little like pride reflected in his eyes. "Look, if you're going to the dance, you better get back. I'm sure Jess is pissed."

"She's going to kill me." I didn't even bother talking to Greg again as I turned and hurried back to the apartment. Within two minutes, I entered through our door.

When I opened the door, Jess stopped pacing, and it felt like her eyes were shooting daggers. "Where the hell have you been?" She was gorgeous. Her eyeshadow nearly matched her dress color and was mere perfection.

"I'm sorry. But we figured out what was wrong with me and my wolf." I walked past her, making my way into her room. My black dress was hanging on the door's hook. I unbuttoned my shirt and removed the jeans I'd been wearing.

"First, we get dressed, then you fill me in." She unzipped the dress and carefully put it over my head. Once it was in place, she zipped it up. "Damn, girl. You look amazing."

I turned to the mirror once again and took a quick breath. I almost didn't recognize myself.

The main door opened and slammed shut. Greg's musky scent hit me hard, and his footsteps stomped down the hallway toward my room and bathroom.

"What's his problem?" Jess placed a hand on her hip.

"He found me with Damien." I guess it did look bad in hindsight, but he was being an asshole. "In the middle of the woods. Alone."

"I bet that hurt his ego." Jess huffed and rolled her eyes. "He must be overcompensating for his little dick."

"Oh my God." I died laughing, which caused my eyes to water.

"No, none of that." Jess pointed her finger in my face. "You will not mess up my masterpiece."

"Okay. Damn." If I didn't stop myself, she might hurt me. I waved my hand in front of my face, letting the air hit my eyes. "See, drying them up right now."

"Good, now let's go." Jess opened her door and marched like a soldier into the den. "We're leaving, Greg."

There was shuffling in the bathroom, and then the door to my bedroom opened. "Okay, sorry. I didn't expect to be gone for so long."

Was he bipolar? His face was calm, and he gave me his usual grin. "You look amazing."

"Thanks?" I hadn't meant for it to come out as a question, but he'd thrown me off with his sudden niceness. It was like we hadn't just run into each other in the woods.

"Okay, let's go." Jess grabbed her bag and opened the door.

It didn't take us long to get to the dance. It was held in the school's main entrance, but someone had hung lights and a disco ball in the center. The lights were low, and there was a DJ in the corner. The room had been emptied of all furniture, and against the wall near the front doors were two tables of drinks. One was labeled blood, and the other was labeled water.

The room didn't even feel like the same one I walked through every day. "This is amazing."

"I know." Jess grinned and seemed to be taking in the room as well.

"This is so much cooler than our dances back at school." Greg watched the dance floor as some of the kids were already out there and grinding on one another.

An earthy smell hit my nose, and I turned, seeking the source. When my eyes landed on Rage, my world seemed to shift, and it felt like I couldn't breathe. He apparently had just gotten here, and his suit hugged his body in all the right places. I couldn't help the arousal that coursed through me.

Soon, his gaze landed on mine, and he began to head in my direction.

"Earth to Rage," Cole called behind him and glanced at Damien. "It's like he's not listening to me. How is that possible?"

"Maybe because you're annoying as hell sometimes." Damien adjusted his tie and groaned.

"You wanna dance?" Greg asked from behind me, but I was at the mercy of Rage's and my connection.

It only took him seconds to finally reach me, but it was like time had stopped.

"You feel it too?" He stopped just a few inches away from me. "It's so damn much stronger than before."

Words were impossible, and all I could do was find the control to nod. If I did anything more, all of my self-control would snap, and I'd be climbing up his chest.

A hand reached from behind grabbed me around the waist to pull me away from Rage.

"Don't fucking touch her." Rage growled and shoved Greg.

"Are you serious?" Greg puffed out his chest and stood his ground.

No matter what happened next, there wasn't going to be a good outcome.

CHAPTER FIFTEEN

The music stopped, and the room was filled with silence. We were making a scene. "Come on, let's go outside."

Both guys were staring at each other, neither one wanting to make the first move.

I raised my voice so it was loud and direct. "Outside. Now." I focused on the front doors and made my way through them. I refused to make more of a scene inside.

"This is kind of exciting," Jess whispered as she followed me. "I mean, I have front row seats to this."

"Seriously?" I wanted Greg gone and now. It took tonight for me to finally see how much of an ass he truly was and how he had treated me. I was a piece of property to him and nothing more.

"Don't get me wrong. I don't want to see you hurt." Jess wrapped an arm around me. "But Rage fighting over a girl was something no one ever thought would happen. There've been so many who tried and hoped for that."

"Stop that sentence right there." It was insane for me to

get angry, thinking of other girls with him. He belonged to me—only me.

The front doors slammed shut as Greg and Rage made their way outside.

Greg's cheap-ass suit was tearing at the seams, and pure hate was written across his face. "Tell him that you're mine."

"I can't do that." I had wanted to give him respect with this inevitable conversation, but he didn't deserve it.

"Raven, tell him that you're mine." Greg's eyes glowed, forcing the alpha power on me.

Whatever he expected, it wasn't going to happen. I didn't see him as my alpha or someone I needed to listen to. Besides, what kind of pathetic person tries to force the alpha connection when it came to claiming a mate?

"Are you fucking kidding me right now?" I was tired of always taking his shit and living in his shadow. "Don't even try that alpha shit on me."

Cole and Damien appeared beside us. I wasn't sure how they got here, but at the moment, that wasn't my concern.

"Is that dickhead really trying to control her?" Damien took off his suit jacket and placed it in the grass.

The last thing I needed was more people trying to get involved. "You know things aren't working out between us."

"I come down here for a surprise visit, and you pull this shit?" Greg took a step closer to me, and Rage growled deep.

"First off, had I known you were coming, I would've told you not to bother." This is what he did, made himself the victim in every circumstance. "You know why I wasn't coming home, so this was just your excuse to get down here."

"You aren't allowed to break up with me." His hands clenched into fists, and his face took on a red hue.

"The hell she's not." Rage forced the words out, visibly trying to maintain some sort of control.

"Yes, I am." I wouldn't stay tied to this damn asshole.

"When did you become such a ..."

A loud, evil laugh escaped from Cole. "Amazing? Strong? Independent? You better be careful choosing the word you use to complete that sentence." Damien stood next to me on the right and Cole on my left.

"If that was true," Greg snarled and glanced at each of them, "then why are you all protecting her?"

"That's the thing. We aren't." Jess lifted her head high and looked down her nose at him. "We are her friends and will do anything to help her."

It was kinda funny. It took her saying that for me to realize she was right. Even Damien was willing to stand by my side.

"This is bullshit." Greg glanced around, and it must have sunk in that he was greatly outnumbered. "I'm out of here, but expect a call from your parents."

"Looking forward to it." A blatant lie, but I couldn't let him know that. Then it hit me. My parents gave me the necklace that was spelled. I wondered if they knew about that. Surely they didn't. My parents wouldn't want to cause me to be imbalanced.

"You will regret this." Greg stomped off and headed toward the parking lot.

As soon as he was out of sight, my shoulders felt a little bit lighter. I hadn't realized the toll he had put on me.

"Thank the gods he's gone." Jess clapped her hands and grabbed my arm. "Let's go and have fun. We haven't missed much of the dance."

"It's time to put our boogie shoes on." Cole did a cheesy two-step.

"You do realize that's a country dance, right?" They were in there blaring the cha-cha, and he was out here line dancing.

"It's the only respectable dance anyone can do." Cole arched an eyebrow and crossed his arms, practically daring me to argue. "We are in the south and must dance as though we are."

Sometimes, I couldn't help but wonder what his parents were like. Sometimes, there was no reasoning with him.

Damien took a step closer to me and whispered in my ear, "See what I was saying earlier."

In his defense, Cole was a bundle of life on his own despite being a vampire. He could be a handful at times. "Yeah." So with the quiet, he could be overwhelming.

"Yeah, you all go on in." Rage frowned at how close Damien was to me. "I need to talk to Raven alone before we go back in."

"Of course." Jess's eyes lit, and she grabbed Cole's arm. "Come on, go two-step with me."

"Hell, yeah." He lifted an arm in celebration. "Finally, someone who understands."

"Are you guys really going to make me go back in with those two?" Damien scowled and huffed.

Poor guy, he looked completely miserable. "Now is that chance you've been looking for to sneak away."

"You're right." He grinned as the door shut behind Cole and Jess. "I'll see you tomorrow."

"Alright, bright and early." Even though it was technically a break day and I'd finally connected with my wolf, I still felt a little volatile and didn't want to go home after what had just happened with Greg.

"Yup, our normal place." He turned quickly and disappeared into the woods, leaving Rage and me alone.

"You're different tonight." Rage still stood where he'd been since we got outside.

"Damien didn't tell you?" I was sure he'd already know.

"No, what?" Rage took a step closer to me. Our connection was like a magnet. It was physically hard not to just wrap my arms around him.

However, I had to stay grounded. I couldn't be jumping him. We had to meet in the middle. "Professor Shaw determined what was causing my wolf and me to be so ... separate."

"Really?" His eyes scanned over me.

"It was my necklace." It still hadn't completely registered with me yet. "He broke the spell, and now we're one."

"Why would someone spell you?" A look of concern crossed his face.

"I ... I don't know." I still didn't understand that part myself. "My mother gave it to me when I was sixteen."

"You think it was her?" He watched me with a guarded expression.

"No, no I don't." My parents wouldn't ever do anything like that. "Mom said she'd found it at a local market, and it reminded her of me." I hoped my voice sounded confident. Honestly, I was kind of wondered if there could be more to the necklace. But my mother wouldn't hide something like that from me... would she?

"Well, I'm damn glad you figured it out." Now he was only a breath away. "It's been driving me crazy." He reached out and touched my face, which caused a warm buzzing sensation. "There it is, finally."

Not able to resist, I placed my hand on his. "What is this?"

"We're true mates." His breath smelled of mint, and my hormones kicked into overdrive.

I had to focus on his words and not his proximity. "Those don't happen anymore." Nowadays, we chose a mate and forced the bond.

"Correction." His eyes focused on my lips. "They are rare, but dammit, I've researched the hell out of it the last six months ... because nothing was making sense about why I'm so drawn to you. Then tonight, when I saw you, I couldn't continue the charade. It has to be because your wolf is free."

"I don't want to get hurt. You have a reputation." The words tumbled from my mouth even though I didn't mean for them to, and I cringed.

"I had one." He lowered his head, hovering over my lips. "I'm yours forever."

There was so much brewing between us that it was hard not closing the distance. Still, for some reason, I needed him to be the one to do it.

Finally, he brushed his lips against mine. It felt like electricity running down my spine, but instead of hurting, it was agonizing. He wasn't close enough. Not near enough.

Responding to his kiss, I deepened it, letting him know I was in for forever as well. When you kissed your fated mate, it really began the bonding. I at least knew that much.

He growled and wrapped his arms around my waist, tugging me close and right up against his arousal. "Damn, you're driving me crazy. Your scent, your taste, this fucking dress."

The door opened, interrupting our moment.

"Raven, I don't give a shit if you guys are making out." Jess hurried over and tugged me away from him. A small smile lifted her lips, but she kept her stern face intact. "You are supposed to be hanging out with me. So inside. Now."

In all reality, I didn't want to leave this moment, but I'd

be a shitty friend if I didn't. "Are you ready to come back in?"

"Sure, let's go." He grabbed my hand, interlocking our fingers.

"So, you guys a thing now?" Jess stayed put, staring Rage down.

"We're more than that," he said as he tugged me close, nearly kissing my lips again. "I'm hers."

She smiled, but there was concern in her eyes. "Well, she's my best friend, so you're gonna share."

"Of course, he will." I untangled myself from him and wrapped my arm around her. "Let's go dance."

"Now that's the spirit." She opened the door, pushing me inside the room.

Cole was in the middle of the dance floor, still doing the two-step with some girl who barely had anything on. She was batting her eyes and giggling with each step he took.

"Oh, my gods." Jess stomped and headed straight to Cole. "I leave for two seconds, and you already have someone else taking my spot."

"Well, she just kinda slipped into my hands and knew the dance." Cole shrugged and disentangled himself from her.

"Hey, I thought we were dancing." The girl pouted and leaned over, allowing her cleavage to be on complete display.

"My friend here does it better and takes priority." He smacked the girl's ass and turned to Jess. "Come on. No time for pouting."

They began dancing together. Rage stepped close, placing his arms around my waist. "She gets you in here and then runs off with him."

"Right, the hussy." I turned around so we were facing

one another. "But I guess this is an acceptable second option."

"Just acceptable?" He arched an eyebrow and pulled me in close. "Guess I need to work on it." He began swaying with me.

"You do realize this isn't a slow dance?" I stepped closer to him, making sure there was no space between us.

"I don't care." He leaned down and kissed my lips. His lips were so soft that it felt like mine melted into his.

"Alright, I'm cutting in." Jordan stood next to us and crossed her arms. "So move." Her hair was in a tight French twist, and she wore a skin-tight red dress with a slit all the way to her upper thigh. It was so low cut there wasn't much left to the imagination. It was amazing that they hadn't been set free by now.

It was like cold water splashed all over me. I pulled back and growled.

"Oh, how cute. The puppy can make noises now." Jordan laughed and grabbed my arm, tugging me away from Rage.

"Don't fucking touch her." Rage's tone was cold.

"Then get her to move." Jordan stared at him. "I'm cutting in."

"No, you're not." He grabbed her arm and scowled. "If you don't let go, I'll make you regret it. Are you really sure you want to mess with me?"

I was so tired of everyone thinking they could treat me like shit. I turned to face her and kicked her right in her stomach. She flew against the wall hard, and her dress tangled up around her legs.

The music stopped, and people began to gather around so they could watch the show.

"You heard him; the answer is no. Now get your ass

moving." I would never play the victim again. It was time to rewrite my story.

"Do you know who you're messing with?" Jordan's eyes glowed, and she untangled herself to get in my face. "You're nothing here. Hell, you can't even bond with your wolf. Step aside, and let me show you how a real woman dances."

Cole appeared on the other side of me, and he tilted his head, examining Jordan. There was a coldness to his face, and he began to advance on her. "Don't pretend you're more than you are." He circled her like she was prey.

"What are you doing? It shouldn't bother you for me to be with him. After all, you threw me aside just like ..." Jordan spat as she pointed to Rage, "... did Ashley. Are you jealous?" Jordan's heart skipped a beat when she took a step back, and Cole countered, getting even closer. "Rage, tell him to stop."

"Do you really think I care about you?" Rage stepped toward her, and I would've protested if I hadn't seen his eyes. He was just as scary as Cole right now, but for some reason, I felt truly protected by both of them. "Do you really think you meant something to Cole or could ever mean something to me?"

"I'm more than either of you will ever be." She stopped moving as they both stalked her.

"Remember, what did I tell you before we started?" Cole narrowed his eyes. "That it was only a fling and not to get attached."

The thought of them being together was disgusting, but I held my tongue. Too much was at stake in this face-off.

"So, it was you who actually pretended we were more." Cole's fangs extended, and a cold smirk crossed his face.

Jordan's breathing became ragged, and she bit her

bottom lip. "But she just started. How is she worthy and I'm not?"

"Because you're just a nobody who pretends to be more." Cole grabbed her arm and pulled her to him. "But you see, there are two things she has that you don't."

"Oh, really?" She was petrified but trying to pretend she wasn't. Her voice was strong, but her whole body was quivering. "Which are?"

"The only thing you need to know," Rage said, standing in front of her, "is that she's something you'll never be. She's my true mate."

"What?" Jordan's mouth dropped open.

The people around us began whispering.

"And that's the only reason you will ever need to know." Cole released her from his grip and scowled. "Now get the hell out of here before I change my mind and finally hit a woman."

She stumbled away, her face turning close to the same shade as a tomato. She caught my eyes though and mouthed the words *you're going to pay*.

Great, now she'd be gunning for me even more than she'd already been.

CHAPTER SIXTEEN

After Jordan made her dramatic exit, the music started once more, but I wasn't in the mood to dance. Between Jordan and Greg, things were sure messy, but my need for Rage overshadowed everything.

"What's wrong?" Rage returned to me with concern written all over his face.

"I just need to be alone with you." I hated feeling this way but couldn't help it.

"Hey." Rage patted Cole on the arm. "We're getting out of here."

"Yeah, I guess we just had the best part of the evening." Cole once again looked like the kind-hearted, inappropriate person I'd come to love. "What are we going to do?"

"No, you and Jess can stay and have fun." Rage wrapped an arm around me. "I want some alone time with Raven."

"I wonder why?" Cole arched an eyebrow.

I wanted to melt into the floor. I couldn't even make eye contact with him.

"What's wrong, Ravey?" Jess wrapped her arms around me, giving me a big hug. "Your face is really flushed."

Cole grinned wide. "Rage just said he …"

"Stop." Rage's features showed indifference, but I could see the edges of his lips trying to break into a smile. "That's enough. I think Raven and I need a little fresh air."

"Fine, but when we meet back up tonight, you're going to have to tell me why you never divulged that Rage was your mate." Jess placed her hands on her hips and stared me down.

"Yes, ma'am." I couldn't help but love that crazy fae.

"Go have fun, be safe." She turned her razor-sharp gaze on Rage. "If you hurt her, I will hunt you down like the dog you are."

"That's it. It's final." Cole chuckled and wrapped his arms around Jess. It was funny because he almost had to bend down to reach her. "She is the fifth member of this pack."

"What? Really?" I'd never seen Jess this happy before. Her grin was nearly bigger than her face, and she hugged Cole back with vigor. "This is the best night ever."

"Alright, now that's all settled, we'll see you guys later." Rage placed his hand at the small of my back and ushered me outside.

The night was beautiful. The moon was half-full, and there wasn't a cloud in the sky. The stars seemed to shine a little brighter than they would normally. A few lightning bugs were buzzing about, making it seem like the stars were twinkling all around us.

"Other than those two odd confrontations, this has been the best night of my entire life." His earthy scent surrounded me, and his words warmed my heart.

For the first time in my life, I felt content. "Me too. I wouldn't change it for the world."

"I hate that we're all leaving in the morning." He sighed and leaned over to kiss me on the forehead.

"Aw, I hadn't even thought of that." Damn, that sucked. I couldn't even fathom the thought, but it wasn't fair to ask him to stay here with me. "What time are you going?"

"Cole is taking me to my pack in Marietta. We're leaving around seven." His dark hair shined in the moonlight, and he was even more breathtaking than normal.

"Really ... when will you be back?" I was hoping for Christmas, but in reality, I knew it would be after New Year's Eve. This was the one time that the Academy allowed us to have a break.

"New Year's Day." He frowned and pulled me against him. "What about you?"

"Oh, I'm staying here." I was kinda surprised that Damien hadn't told him.

"What do you mean you're staying here?" His forehead wrinkled as he pulled me around so I was facing him.

"Isadora isn't allowing me to go back home because I'm so out of sync with my wolf." It was strange that this wasn't common knowledge.

"So, what are you supposed to do?" His hands touched the bare skin of my back, causing the warm buzzing to take over my senses.

"Damien is staying to train me over the break."

"At least he's one I trust." His lips touched mine, and the conversation we were having seemed to fade away.

He picked me up like a damsel in distress and began walking but still not breaking the kiss.

I giggled, not able to help myself. "Where are we going?"

"You'll see when we get there." He lowered his mouth to mine once more, and I relaxed in his arms, enjoying the moment. Before long, we were in the boy's dormitory.

"Am I even allowed to be here?" I whispered the words, afraid someone would spot us any second.

"Yes, you're fine. Both Cole and I have been in your room."

"Oh, yeah." It always felt normal to have them there. I never once considered whether we could have guys in our rooms.

"You're so damn cute and innocent." He passed the elevators and continued down the hall.

We turned down a hallway that had four doors on each side. He continued down the hall, stopping at the last one on the right. "Alright, here we are." He bent and gently placed me so that both of my feet were on the ground. He pulled a key out of his pocket and unlocked the door. "Welcome to my humble abode."

As I entered, the scents of cotton candy, pine, and earth filled the den. "You're roommates with Cole or Damien?"

"Both." His den and kitchen were larger than ours, but other than that, it appeared the same. He pointed down the hallway on the left. "This is where my room is, and the right hall is where Damien and Cole's are."

"Wait, they sleep together?" I didn't get that kind of vibe from the two of them.

"Hell, no." Damien stepped out of the hallway Rage had just pointed down. "There are two bedrooms off this hall, and each has its own bathroom. I want to make that very clear." He had already changed out of his suit and was dressed in a pair of gray pajama bottoms and a shirt. "The only reason why Rage got that one was because he got to the academy first."

"But you're not bitter at all." Rage headed into the kitchen and opened the fridge. He pulled out a beer and took a swig.

"Nope." Damien glanced in my direction and cleared his throat. "You never bring girls here. Why now, and why her? You know I'm training her."

"Don't worry. This is different." Rage gazed at me tenderly. "Do you want anything to drink?"

"No, I'm good. Thanks."

"Look, I know you got the hots for Rage. I've known it from day one, but you need to think this through." Damien sighed and ran his hand through his hair. "I don't want things to get awkward between us later."

Ahh. His concern made sense now.

"It won't be an issue." Rage took another swig and made his way back to me, wrapping his arm around my waist. "She's my mate, Damien."

"What?" Damien's brows furrowed, and he looked confused.

"We're true mates." I felt like I had to say something. Rage had been doing all the talking. "So, he can't get rid of me."

"Well, thank the gods." He moved to the couch and sat down on it. "I thought you two acted really strange around each other. It must have finally clicked when your block was removed tonight."

"Yeah, that's what I figured too." I glanced down and played with the hem of my dress.

An awkward silence descended when Damien finally stood and chuckled. "Well, I need to run to the main building for a while and make sure nothing crazy happened. I had just gotten a text from Isadora before you two came in." He stood and moved past me. "I'll be back later."

"Hey, you're in pajama pants." I didn't want him to go out and embarrass himself.

"I hate to tell you this, but once my PJs are on, there's no taking them off until the morning." He opened the door and glanced at me. "She knows what she's getting."

When the door shut, Rage turned me around and kissed me. His mouth tasted of mint and beer, something I never would've imagined I'd like, but it was delicious. He picked me up and hoisted me so that I could wrap my legs around his waist. He carried me into his bedroom and placed me on his bed. He stood and stared at me. "Damn, you're beautiful." He locked the door and then climbed over me, placing some of his weight against me. "We don't have to do anything if you don't want to."

"No, it's not that. It's just Ash ..."

He placed a finger over my lips. "I can't take away my past, but I'll tell you one thing. No one has ever been in my bed."

Some of the tension released from my body, and when he kissed me again, there was no hesitation. I kissed him back and pulled him down closer to me.

His hands grabbed my waist, digging his fingers into me.

A groan escaped me, but I didn't give a damn. I sucked on his tongue as his hands made their way to my breasts. He slipped them under the top of my dress, rubbing just the right way. I never felt so close to someone before and I never wanted this to end.

I clung to him even tighter until I felt his hardness, and I began rubbing myself against it.

"Damn, I don't want to go fast." He kissed down my neck, lower and lower, until he reached my breasts, sucking on them.

My hands grabbed at his jacket, yanking it off. He

raised so he could get his arms out of the sleeves. While he was up, I ripped his button-down shirt, pushing it off at the same time.

When I was able to see his glorious chest, it only turned me on even more. Every muscle was well defined and sexy as hell.

He grabbed my waist and flipped me over, unzipping my dress. He slipped the material over my hips and kissed every inch of flesh on the way down.

As he reached my panties, he kissed the inside of my legs. In that moment, everything had changed. He was the man I always wanted and didn't know. There had been enough foreplay, and I needed him now, needed him to claim me.

I flipped back around and grabbed the waist of his slacks, quickly unbuttoning his pants. I pulled them and his boxers off at the same time. He was as ready as I was.

"You know, this is the final thing. We're mated. No ceremony needed. You're mine if we do this. Forever." He climbed back on top of me and looked into my eyes. "Are you sure?"

"Of course I am." As soon as those words left my lips, he plunged into me over and over again. Our souls connected and everything fell into place.

Pushing him over, I climbed on top and rode him. He was now hitting deeper and deeper until I came unglued.

We both groaned as our muscles contracted, and I fell against his chest.

"Are you okay?" He laughed and pulled me close.

"More than okay." That was the best sex I'd ever experienced. "Are you?"

"This has been the best moment of my entire existence. Now I don't have just a true mate; I have a bonded mate." He kissed my lips and started doing it all over again.

Rage's phone kept buzzing.

"Don't you think you should answer that?" We'd lost count of how many times we'd been together, and I wouldn't have it any other way.

"Yeah, I guess so. We need to get moving anyway. I'm sure Cole will be here any second. He leaned over to pick up his underwear and pants before pulling them on. He grabbed the phone and groaned. "Get dressed. We have to go."

I jumped out of bed, quickly pulling my panties and dress back on. My hair was a mess, but there was no way to fix that here. "What's wrong?"

"Isadora wants to see us." He groaned and put the phone in his pocket.

"Is everything okay?" I'd never been called to the headmaster's office before. It had to be everything I messed up with Greg and Jordan. Ugh, this felt like being called to the principal's office.

He grabbed his shirt and then chuckled. "So, there's no salvaging this."

"Uh ... sorry?" There wasn't anything more I could say than that even though I really wasn't.

"I'm not." He walked over and kissed my lips. "Alright, the longer we wait the worse it'll get." He moved to his closet and grabbed another shirt. This time, it was a white polo and not a button-down.

"What did we do?" I wasn't sure what to expect. I'd never gotten in trouble before.

"Don't worry. Jordan probably ran over to complain that we were bullying her." He grabbed my hand, pulling me out the door. "But the thing is, we would've never done that if she hadn't caused a scene. I'm sure she left out that important part, so we just have to go and tell Isadora what really happened."

It didn't take long for us to reach her office. I'd never been in it before, but it was one place I'd never forget. The floor was a dark pine, and there was a large dark cherry wood bookcase that took up the whole wall. In the center of it was a cut out entirely filled with a painting of a woman that very much favored the woman who was sitting at a huge desk placed in front of it. The desk seemed to be made of the same dark cherry wood as the bookcase with a large leather desk chair sitting behind it. She had four seats in front of the desk, which were already occupied by Jess, Cole, and Damien.

"So nice of you two to join us." Isadora was sitting in the chair right behind the desk. Her sparkling green eyes seemed to rake up and down me. "We've been trying to get in touch with you both for a while now."

"I'm sorry about that." Rage tensed but refused to let go of my hand.

"No excuses then?" She leaned back in her chair and placed her two index fingers under her chin.

"It was my fault." I refused to let Rage take the blame.

Cole chuckled and elbowed Damien. "It takes two to tango."

"Will you two shut up?" Jess grinned but at least pretended to be offended by what Cole had just said.

"Two?" Damien shook his head. "I believe Cole was the only one talking. I always get lumped in with you two even when I'm not involved in your shit."

"You're known for who you hang out with." Cole swayed his index fingers Damien's way.

"Will you cut the shit?" Isadora glared at Cole as she stood. "Now, Ms. Wright and Mr. Jackson, please come in and join us."

Rage placed his hand on the small of my back and guided me to take the chair. I wanted to argue with him, but I wasn't going to test Isadora's patience.

"I was informed of a very public disturbance tonight." She paced behind her desk with a frown that seemed to be permanently placed. "It involved two of my most influential students."

"Oh, come on. It was that bitch Jordan causing shit again." Cole slumped in his seat and groaned.

"If you want to act like a toddler, then I shall treat you like one." She slammed her hand on the desk, and her teeth extended.

"With all due respect, I have to agree with Cole on this one." Damien closed his eyes and grimaced. "Jordan and Ashley have taken a keen interest in not only Cole and Rage but Raven as well."

"I bet that hurt to admit," Jess whispered, but with all of the supernatural ears in the room, every single one of us heard her.

"Traitor." Cole crossed his arms, somehow sinking even further into the chair.

"So, tell me your version of what happened tonight?" Isadora arched an eyebrow, and her eyes landed on me.

"Oh, well Damien texted me to tell me ..."

Rage interrupted me. "I was dancing with Raven and Jordan tried to cut in."

Her eyes cut to Rage. "Pray tell, what was the problem with that?"

"I'd just discovered that Raven was my mate, and I didn't want to leave her."

Isadora breathed deeply. "True mate?"

"Yes, we were connecting, and she interfered." Rage touched the back of my chair, leaning against me. "We explained that to Jordan, and she wouldn't let up."

"Well, she did ask for it this time, I suppose." She sat in the chair and crossed her legs. "However, this cannot be a common occurrence, or there will be repercussions. I have too much at stake with another issue. I don't have time to deal with your toddler-like antics. Am I clear?"

"Of course." Damien stood and headed to the door, opening it.

"Don't worry, Izzy." Cole jumped from his chair and winked at her. "We won't let you down."

"For the last time, Mr. Weston, my name is Isadora, not Izzy." Her eyes began sparkling again, but there was still an edge to her tone.

"You can't blame me for getting it confused." Cole grabbed Jess's hand and pulled her up. He wrapped an arm around her and pointed at Isadora. "Night, Izzy. Make sure you get some rest." They both walked out the door as the headmaster sighed.

As I neared the door, Isadora cleared her throat. "Oh, and Miss Wright?"

I paused and turned around. "Yes?"

Rage passed through the door but stopped at the threshold.

"Professor Shaw informed me that you had some kind

of block on your wolf and that you are now as one." She tapped her fingers together and paused. "Make sure you get it under control before the others come back from winter vacation. If not, I'll have to take things into my own hands."

Great, not only do I have two girls who are out to get me, but the headmaster just threatened me again. I wasn't sure how I was going to survive this school.

CHAPTER SEVENTEEN

It felt lonely staying in my apartment without Jess tinkering around. I was already missing Rage even though he'd only been gone for two hours. When did I turn into this girl?

I made my way into the kitchen and got a glass of water. I'd barely gotten any sleep, especially after our meeting with Isadora. Rage promised me that everything would be fine. He thought that since everyone knew I was his mate and that Cole was loyal to me; things would begin to slow down. But I wasn't so sure. I might've synced with my wolf, but I still had so much to learn.

A knock at the door froze me in my tracks. Maybe I had just jinxed myself. I tiptoed over to the door, looking through the peephole.

"Rave, just open the damn door already. I can smell you right there." Damien sighed and knocked on the door again.

Damn, I really needed to get my head in the game or I wouldn't survive. Not even bothering with a response, I unlocked the door and opened it.

"Who the hell did you think I was?" Damien put his hands in the pockets of his jeans.

"You'll say I'm overreacting just like Rage said before he left." I hated this feeling of being a walking target. "It's not that I don't trust him, but there's something about both Ashley and Jordan that's bothering me."

"There is no doubt that they're going to come after you." He leaned against the edge of the door. "That's why we need to make sure you're in control, especially now that you're one with your wolf."

The fact that he agreed with me completely threw me off my game. "What?" Wow, I was being so very eloquent here.

"I said I agreed with you." Damien chuckled. "Rage has an inflated ego at times. He has a god tendency even if he has good intentions. Those girls are vicious and obviously want you dead."

It was nice for someone to be on my side. "But my wolf and I are merged. Doesn't that solve everything?"

"No, it doesn't. You still have to feel out your bond." He scanned me from top to bottom. "I'm honestly surprised I didn't find you in your pajamas."

"If only you'd come like five minutes earlier." It was odd, but somehow all three of those guys had made their way into my heart. Rage would've regardless, for obvious reasons, but not the other two. Somehow, they'd managed it all on their own.

"Thank goodness I didn't. Since I don't think Rage would be very happy with me." His gaze went to the den. "Go get a couple changes of clothes. I don't need Rage killing me before I get to ring in the New Year."

Not arguing, I ran into my room and grabbed a bag,

piling it with three changes of clothes. He said a couple, but I figured an extra outfit might be warranted. Better to have extra and not need it than the opposite.

"Alright, I'm ready." I threw the pink zipper bag over my shoulder.

We made our way to the first floor and out the door.

"Let's go to our usual spot." Damien led the way, and we moved in amicable silence.

When we reached the clearing, he paused. "Now, we need to do things differently here. It's not going to be like the last time."

"Okay, let's do this." I figured there was no point in being negative. I threw my bag on the ground.

"Alright, we're going to recreate the very first night you got here, but I want you to not shift." He walked across the opening and slid behind some trees.

Overall, shifters aren't uncomfortable with nudity, but we still didn't go out of our way to have our dangly bits on display for everyone to see.

A loud roar broke through the silence, and all my instincts kicked into gear.

It didn't take long for Damien in his large grizzly form to come racing into the clearing. He pawed at the ground, and his eyes landed on me. He roared once more before charging toward me.

Even though I knew this was an exercise, it felt real. He looked pissed. My bones began to crack as the shift pressed upon me.

No, this can't happen. Damien told me to control myself and not let this happen. I took a deep breath, trying to remain calm. However, another bone cracked, and my hands grew fur. No, dammit. I thought this would be easy.

When he was within ten feet of me, his mouth opened wide, revealing his sharp teeth with drool dripping out the sides. He stood on his hind feet, ready to fight.

That's all it took for the shift to happen. My clothes ripped, and fur sprouted all over me. I howled and prepared to attack.

Damien then dropped to all fours, and every ounce of aggression vanished. He ran back in the direction he'd come from to shift back.

It pissed me off that I'd shifted. I thought there wouldn't be any problem for me to remain human. With my teeth, I grabbed the strap of my bag and dragged it behind two large trees. I shifted back and chose a gray shirt and black yoga pants. I dressed quickly and met Damien back in the clearing.

"Ugh, I messed up." I hated that I failed.

"To be honest, you did better than I expected." He gave me one of his rare grins. "I almost thought you weren't going to shift."

"It was a struggle." More than I liked to admit. "But at least I didn't blackout like that first night."

"That's the point of this exercise." He picked a twig from his hair. "If it were easy, then we wouldn't need to work on it."

"You're right." Isadora's threat rang in my ears. "Okay, I'm ready to try again."

Pride seemed to gleam from his eyes. "Alright then, let's try again." He turned and ran back to the area across from me. He slipped between two trees and disappeared.

Okay, I have to concentrate more and be in control. I threw my arms to each side and jogged in place.

Damien appeared again in his bear form, but when his

eyes landed on me, his big grizzly mouth lifted at the corners. It seemed like he was laughing.

Great, even in animal form, I was being made fun of. I stilled and waited for the inevitable attack. "What are you laughing at? At least when I shift, I don't smell like ass." Damnit. Maybe I shouldn't be poking at the big ass bear.

He roared loud and began a quick run toward me. He could run fast for such a large animal.

The adrenaline pulsed inside me, and my body once again wanted to shift. I closed my eyes, trying to block out his attack. However, his heavy breathing and loud steps seemed to echo in my ears. The closer he got, the harder it was to ignore.

When it felt like he was right on me, my eyes popped open, and my bones began to crack all on their own accord. I tried to hold it back, but it felt like my body was fighting against me. All too quickly, I lost control. My bones broke, and the ground seemed to drop out from under my feet as I shrank once again, back into my wolf form.

My breathing was ragged, and I whined in frustration. All this seemed to knock the strength out of me. Ugh, I messed up again.

For the next week, every day played out the same way. Damien and I would head to the same spot, and over and over again, I failed. The only good news was it did seem as if I was gaining some control, but still not anywhere near what I needed to have.

I grabbed a cup of coffee from my Keurig and made my way to the couch. Damien's family apparently didn't live far away, so he was spending Christmas morning with them, leaving me alone in my apartment. He'd offered to take me with him, but it would've made the wrong impression. Going to a guy's house on Christmas to spend time with him and his family just felt wrong since it wasn't Rage.

Of course, I missed that man too damn much. We'd talked every night, but it wasn't the same as him being here with me. It was amazing that I'd met my mate, my true mate, but I hated that he had to leave the very next day.

My phone rang, so I grabbed it from the table in front of me. Of course, it would be my parents. I wished more than anything I could be there with them. However, Isadora wanted me here until my wolf and I were in complete sync with one another. I couldn't be out and about feeling threatened and shift in front of humans. "Hey."

"Merry Christmas." My parents both said in unison.

"Aw, Merry Christmas." Hearing their voices tugged on my heart even more.

"We miss you, baby girl." My dad's voice was strained as if he was trying not to cry.

"I miss y'all too." They both meant the world to me. I reached for my necklace and grasped air. "I'm sorry I couldn't make it home."

"We know it's not your fault." Mom's tone had an edge for some reason. "Still, you never told us a specific excuse for not coming home for Christmas."

For some reason, my gut told me not to tell her, at least for now. I didn't suspect my parents had anything to do with the necklace and its block, but I needed to figure out who spelled it before I tell them what happened. Speaking of which, I needed to get it back from Professor Shaw. "Just struggling with my wolf still, and that causes a risk for anyone I'm around. Especially if I leave here." That was the truth, so I wasn't lying, just omitting certain details.

"Maybe being around family would help you." Mom's voice got higher.

"Liz ..." Dad was always the peacemaker in our family.

Mom and I were very similar, which caused us to fight with each other. Now that I'd been here, I realized she had alpha running in her blood as well. It was a shame that she didn't utilize it.

With the way Mom was acting, I decided I needed to get off the phone with her and fast. I knew it was going to turn into an argument otherwise. "Hey, guys, I've got to run."

"Okay, honey. We just wanted to let you know that we miss you." Dad was quick to speak first. "When you get back home, we'll celebrate Christmas."

Damien had told me we get a week's break in the summer, so it wouldn't be a full year before I saw them again. Just the thought of that break was comforting. "I love you both. Bye." I hung up as tears sprung from my eyes.

I'd never felt alone like this before. If I'd been home, we would've opened gifts and even had breakfast together. Now, I was sitting here all alone with cold seeping throughout my body. Not only had I kept the secret about the necklace, but I hadn't even told my parents about Rage yet either. I figured there was plenty of time for that.

A loud knock rapped against the door.

That man was ruthless and wouldn't give up. "Damien, I told you I wasn't going to your family event." I jumped to my feet and reached the door, swinging it open.

It was Rage.

I jumped into his arms and wrapped my legs around

him. I missed him so damn much. "What are you doing here?"

"Isn't it obvious?" He hugged me tightly. "I couldn't stay away from you any longer, and I couldn't miss our first Christmas together."

It'd only been a week, but it felt like years. Tears glistened in my eyes. "I'm so glad you're here."

"Hey, it's okay." Rage rubbed my back and gently placed me on the ground.

"So now your parents hate me." I sniffed and tried wiping the tears away from my eyes.

"Not at all." He leaned down and kissed my lips. "Mom said she'd been expecting this ever since I told them I found my true mate and that she wasn't allowed off-campus."

"I hate that I sound so weak." This year had never made me feel so insecure and brave at the same time. I needed to move more into the braver side.

"My Dad said that only the strongest suffer like you are." He placed his forehead against mine. "He said that when he went here, there was a girl that was struggling in the same ways as you. Her wolf was so strong she had to be trained to keep both sides of herself in check. They had such high expectations of her, but when her mate got hurt, she left with him instead."

"They just let her go?" That didn't sound like the Isadora I had met since being at the academy.

"Actually, it was the exact opposite." His woodsy scent surrounded me. "Apparently, Professor Shaw and Isadora refused to let her go, but she slipped out one night, never to be seen again."

"Well, of course she would." A mate was the strongest bond formed between our kind.

"Of course. But the strange thing was Isadora tried

finding her over the years, and she's not even a blip on her radar." Rage shrugged and kissed me once more. "Enough of that shit. It's the present." He pulled a small package from his jacket and handed it to me. It was wrapped in shiny blue paper with snowmen all over it. "Open it." A huge grin filled his face.

It still caught me off guard when he smiled like that. I was lucky to be the one who got to receive those. "Well, come in first." I giggled and ran back to the couch, diving onto it. I needed to see what this was pronto.

He shut the door and chuckled. "You're not excited at all, are you?"

"Nope, but out of obligation, I'm trying to humor your male ego." I tore the paper off and found a jewelry type box. He better not have spent a ton of money on me. As I opened the lid, a necklace came into view. It was a silver necklace with a large ruby pendant outlined by a silver edge. "It's gorgeous."

"I figured since the Professor took your moon necklace, you might need a replacement." He glanced at the ground as his cheeks took on a pink hue.

"It's perfect." I'd never seen anything so beautiful. I gently held the necklace and lifted it. The light shone off the ruby pendant, making it even more beautiful. "I love it. Thank you."

"You're welcome." He took the necklace from my hands and twirled his finger around. "Let me put it on you."

"There was no need for you to spend so much on me." I lifted my hair and turned so he could slip it around my neck.

"Don't worry about it." He hooked it and placed a hand on my shoulder. "It's a family heirloom."

Meaning it was worth even more than I realized. "Are you sure …"

He sat next to me, and his eyes landed on the pendant that laid against my chest. "Positive. And it was made for you."

Now, I was even more nervous about the gift I had made him. "One second, let me go grab yours."

"Okay." The side of his mouth twitched upward. "Hurry back."

I ran into my bedroom and grabbed the gift out of the closet. I just hoped that the string art I made of Tennessee would be something he'd like. It did take me several days to make it, which was good since I'd been bored this past week.

As I walked into the room, Rage's eyes landed on it. He stood and took it from my hands. I had placed a heart where we first met. "The heart is your hometown, isn't it?"

"Yes, even then I felt something for you. I just didn't realize the magnitude until my wolf and I merged." To think what I would've missed out on had I not come here.

"When my eyes landed on you, there was no way in hell I would have left without you." He reached over and tucked some of my hair behind my ear. "I'm just glad we got it all sorted out. It was unimaginably hard those six months, not being with you."

"At least we don't have to worry about it now." There was no way I'd be going anywhere without him.

"When is your next training session with Damien?" Rage leaned back against the sofa and pulled me into his arms.

"Tomorrow. He's spending today with his family." Having Rage here with me helped the loneliness I had felt earlier disappear. Just being with him made this the best Christmas I'd ever had before.

"Do you mind if I go with you?" Rage kissed the side of my face as his fingers gently trailed over my arm.

The thought of him watching me fail tore at me, but maybe he could help me. "No, but I hate for you to see me struggling."

"Nothing will ever change how I feel about you." He kissed me once more.

He was right. We were mates. If anything, we should have been stronger together. "Okay." I turned my head so my mouth captured his and deepened the kiss. Soon his hands were running up my sides and slipping under my shirt. I groaned with need for him; needing more.

I lifted myself and wrapped my legs around his waist. He was already hard, wanting me just as much as I wanted him. I slipped my shirt over my head, and he gasped when he realized I wasn't wearing a bra.

"You're going to kill me." He lowered his head, suckling my breasts, and unconsciously I began to grind against him.

"Now." I didn't want slow and steady. No, I wanted fast and hot. I grabbed the waist of his blue jeans and unbuttoned them. "Off, now." I couldn't take them off myself, not with me sitting on him. I slipped off, and he happily obliged by removing his pants and underwear. He reached over and yanked my yoga pants to the ground and grabbed my hips placing me back on top.

Not wasting any time, he entered me. I rode him hard until our muscles began to contract. He leaned down placing my breast in his mouth, causing everything to feel even better. Ecstasy took over as we both climaxed together. "Oh, gods."

"You are so damn hot." He kissed me again, ready to go for yet another round already. And that was how we spent the rest of Christmas Day.

Hushed voices startled me from my sleep. I reached across, looking for Rage, but that side of my bed was cold. He hadn't been lying here for quite a while.

"The other night, I saw more people wearing cloaks coming out from the woods." Damien's all too familiar voice was part of the whispering, which meant Rage had to be the other.

I quickly threw on clothes and headed into the den.

They were sitting in silence when I entered. "What's going on?"

"Nothing." Rage patted the seat next to him. "Damien and I were just catching up."

Damien was in the kitchen, but his arms were crossed. "You ready for training?"

"Yes, our time is almost up." I leaned into Rage, and he wrapped his arm around my shoulders.

"You still okay with me going?" Rage kissed my lips.

"Yeah, as long as Damien approves." I grinned and glanced at Damien.

"It might help since he's another wolf. So maybe he'll understand what you're going through more than me." Damien handed me a coffee and protein bar when he walked by the couch. "Eat up, and let's go."

Rage smirked at our interaction. "Damien, you're getting soft."

"Shut it." Damien glared at Rage. "She needs focus and energy. That's it." He sighed and stretched out his back. "Besides, we need to be careful."

"Careful about what?" It must have something to do with what they were talking about earlier before I came in.

Rage gave him a warning look. "You getting a handle on

your wolf." He grinned, but there was something off in his eyes. He bopped my nose. "You're our number one priority."

He was hiding something from me, and I didn't like that. Something was definitely wrong.

CHAPTER EIGHTEEN

As we headed toward the woods, both Rage and Damien were being extra cautious. I watched them glance around as if something were about to attack us. "What's going on?"

"Nothing," Rage said as he intertwined my fingers with his. "Just being cautious, that's all."

"You normally aren't cautious." It was kind of cute that he thought he could hide things from me. I was willing to play the obedient and quiet girl part for a short time, but not too much longer.

Damien snorted. "She has you there."

"You better watch it." Rage arched his eyebrow at his friend. "I'll start telling everyone all your secrets."

"Do you think that scares me?" Damien rolled his eyes. "You've got nothing."

We reached the clearing, and I dropped my bag of clothes on the ground beside me.

"How many outfits did you bring this time?" Damien glanced at the bag.

He must have noticed it was twice as packed. "I'm

determined to get this today, so I brought ten changes of clothes." That was one of the nice things about living here. They ensured our wardrobes were complete for casual days, uniforms, pajamas, and even a few sets of nice dress clothes for special occasions. They restocked our clothes, wanting all of us to appear put together and strong. However, we were still free to buy other things if we desired.

"You're going to kill this." Rage gently squeezed our connected hands.

"Let's try not to kill me in the process, okay?" Damien shook his head as he ran across the woods, slipping between the trees just like last time.

The anticipation of Damien running out was sometimes worse than when he appeared. I moved away from Rage, needing to concentrate. I rubbed my fingers together and then popped my neck.

Within seconds, Damien roared and came barreling toward me.

He hadn't done that before, so it caused my adrenaline to pump even harder. I took deep breaths, trying to calm down, but it didn't help.

As he approached, he stood on his hind legs and growled once more.

Once again, my limbs began to crack, and fur covered my body. Dammit, I messed up again.

I grabbed my bag with my teeth and dragged it behind a tree so I could change back and dress. I didn't know why I wasn't getting this. Once I was dressed, I headed back out to where Rage was waiting. "Did he already go back?"

"Yeah, but he's going to wait for my call before we try this again." Rage's hand reached out and brushed my cheek. "When he charges you, what are you thinking?"

"I'm thinking I can't shift. That he's not attacking me, that it's all a ruse."

He nodded his head and sighed. "That's your problem."

"Okay, what am I supposed to be thinking?" I sounded like a newly shifted wolf and hated it.

"There will be times when you don't know if someone is a friend or foe." He grabbed my hands and opened them. "You don't want to show your fear in either situation. So instead of concentrating on not shifting, focus on what your next move would be."

"So instead, get a defensive plan ready?" Okay, that kind of made sense. Here I was thinking I shouldn't shift because he won't hurt me even if it sure as hell seemed that way. Maybe having a plan would make me feel better and more in control.

"Exactly." His dark eyes seemed to warm as he watched me.

"Okay, got it." I stretched my arms and took one more deep breath, preparing for the attack. "Ready."

Rage let out an ear-piercing whistle, and within seconds, Damien came barreling toward me.

This time, I thought if he didn't stop and got within two feet of reaching me, I'd kick him in the nuts. I figured that should distract him long enough for me to shift and attack in my animal form.

I watched as he took each step, progressing closer and closer to me. For once, I didn't feel like the prey but the predator.

He roared and stood on his hind legs. Within seconds, he was right in front of me, and the urge to shift wasn't taking control.

Another roar echoed in my ears as Damien bent down,

leaning his bear right in my face. His breath smelled rancid and made my stomach gurgle.

"Dude, you need to brush your teeth." I fanned my hand in front of my face. "Like really bad."

Damien closed his mouth and lowered his body, putting all four paws on the ground. He huffed and then turned to run away.

"That was perfect." Rage laughed as he stepped next to me and turned me around so I could face him. "See, I knew you'd get it." He kissed my lips and pulled back.

"With your help." I wasn't going to lie. I was pretty happy with myself right then.

"I just planted the idea," he said as he tapped my forehead with his index finger. "You're the one who accomplished it."

The trees across the clearing moved as Damien appeared in his fully clothed human form. "You did it."

"Thank goodness. I was getting nervous that I wasn't going to get it." The headmaster's warning echoed in my mind again. Isadora seemed like a woman who kept her word and was a hard ass. I didn't want to end up on her shit list. "Rage gave me a suggestion that worked."

"So now we need to practice your fighting." Damien glanced around and then back at Rage. "Let's end training for today. We can start that tomorrow. You're progressing very nicely."

So tomorrow, my real training begins.

"Now go for his throat," Rage yelled as Damien's bear stood on his hind legs.

My eyes focused on Damien's neck, his weak point. As I

lowered to the ground, I jumped as high as my wolf legs would allow. However, as I was within two inches of his neck, Damien used one of his arms, slamming me into the ground.

I slid across the grass until colliding into a tree. Damn, that really hurt. Still, I refused to show weakness.

As Damien turned around heading for his section across the clearing, I ran quietly and leaned down, nipping at his legs, causing him to lose his balance and fall to the ground.

"Hell, yeah." Rage laughed and ran over to me, stroking my white fur.

It felt amazing being petted by him in this form. His fingers combed easily through my fur.

Damien got back on his paws, but there was a limp to his right hind leg. He growled and turned, heading to where he changed.

"Well, it looks like he has had enough." Rage dropped his hand to his side and chuckled. "Why don't you go get changed while I check on him?"

I nodded and sprinted back toward my clothes. After I was dressed, I waited on the other two to hurry up.

When they both appeared, Damien limped even in his human form.

"I'm so sorry. I didn't mean to hurt you like that." My side still ached from the tree, so maybe it was karma kicking his ass.

"Well, in that form, I'm around six hundred pounds, so falls hurt." He sighed, but there was no malice in his eyes. "Sorry for pushing you like I did. You hit that tree hard, but you bounced back, which was perfect.

"My mate is amazing." Rage kissed my lips and took my hand.

"Okay, none of that here." Damien rolled his eyes but

winked at me. "The best thing you could do for your mate is to not tell her what to do where I can hear you."

"Yeah, it just kinda fell out." Rage cringed and dodged a low hanging branch.

"No worries." I didn't want him to feel bad. "I still brought him down in the end."

"That you did." Damien limped behind us but was still keeping pace.

"How about we go back to my room, and I'll stick some pizzas in the oven?" Between those two and myself, we could eat a full pizza each, if not more.

"That sounds good to me." Damien stumbled over some roots but grabbed a tree branch to keep his balance. He was never this clumsy, so it had to be his injury.

"Hey, I'm really ..."

"Don't apologize." Rage squeezed my hand and grinned. "This place is called Bloodshed for a reason."

"He's right. Besides, I've had way worse injuries." Damien hobbled, but his limp was already improving. "I heal fast, similar to a wolf, so don't worry."

When we stepped inside the apartment, a loud squeal filled the air. All of a sudden, a small body collided with mine. "I've missed you so much."

"I figured you'd be home." The break had flown by fast, and classes began once again the next day. "I've missed you too." I pulled my best friend even closer, hugging her back.

A door from Jess's room opened, and the all too familiar cotton candy scent infiltrated my nose. "I've died and gone to heaven. Did I miss the first kiss yet?"

Of course, Cole's mind would be in the gutter first thing. "Nope, you haven't."

"Hot damn." He clapped his hands and ran into the

kitchen. "I know blood is my usual sustenance, but I think this situation calls for popcorn."

"I hate to tell you this, but I'm not down for my mate being with anyone else but myself." Rage pinched the bridge of his nose and shook his head.

"In full transparency, I don't swing both ways." We hadn't been around Cole for weeks, and it's like he came back fully charged. "So, this whole conversation was pointless."

"Aw, are you having a Betty White moment?" Cole opened the pantry and began shuffling through the shelves. "We may have a problem. There are no Snickers here. Alert. Alert. No Snickers."

"I don't think I can handle this right now?" Damien began inching toward the door.

"If you leave now, there's no telling what might happen to you tonight while you sleep." Cole wagged his eyebrows.

"He's been in rare form, waiting on you three." Jess shrugged and yawned. "You have no clue what I had to endure."

"I think I may have a clue." He was always a handful, so it wasn't hard to imagine. "But he did pick up on me being hangry, which was one hundred percent accurate. "We just got through training and are now ready to cook some pizzas."

"Oh, I'm so craving Slice Pizzeria." Jess jumped up and down. "Let's go out while we still can."

That didn't sound so terrible. I'd rarely been off-campus, so doing something in town wouldn't be bad. "I'm good with that."

"Alright, let's go." Cole pulled out his keys and swung them in the air. "First one there drives the Audi."

Dear gods, no. I didn't know if I could handle his driving again. We all turned and raced out the door.

"There is no way in hell that's going to happen." Jess's wings magically appeared, not even tearing her clothes. They were a translucent silver with magic dust sparkling in the air all around them. She began flapping her wings and vanished from sight almost instantly.

"Did you see that?" My eyes had to be playing tricks on me.

"Yes." Rage stood there blinking. "I can't say I was expecting that."

"Well, I'm pretty sure we don't have a chance of winning." Jess was sure full of surprises. She kept me on my toes.

"Nope, so I say we just take our time." Rage opened the door and bowed. "After you, mi' lady."

"We're being formal now?" When he did stuff like that, it made me swoon. Although I could never let him know willingly. I slipped past him, entering the hall.

"Just need to treat my mate with the love and respect she deserves." He placed his hand on the small of my back and guided me toward the elevators.

"Uh, oh. What did you do?" I loved giving him a hard time.

"If you're that suspicious of me, then I haven't been giving you the proper attention you really need." He grabbed my waist, pulling me in until I pushed against him. "Maybe I should remedy that right now."

"Promises, promises." My body came alive, and I needed his lips on mine.

He lowered his lips to mine, and his tongue teased, asking for entrance. I moaned as I opened my mouth.

"Excuse me." The pretentious voice I'd hope to never hear again filled my ears.

Rage froze and pulled back with a growl. "What's your problem?"

"Two people frisking each other in the hallway. That's what." Ashley squared her shoulders and glared at me.

"Come on." She wasn't worth our time. She was miserable and only wanted to ruin our day. "The others are waiting on us anyway."

He sighed and took a step back, releasing me. "Fine, but we will continue this later."

"Of course." I ignored Ashley and passed her as she probably dreamed of my demise.

Within minutes, we were out in the parking lot. Jess's wings had disappeared, and she flipped her hair over her shoulders. "Give me the keys, Cole. A challenge is a challenge."

"We've never seen your wings before though. Who knew how freakishly fast you are?" Cole clutched onto his keys like a toddler with his toys. "Had I known you were faster than me, I would've said the second person to the car would get to drive. So, really, you're at fault here."

"Just because I don't flaunt my abilities around like a peacock strutting his feathers doesn't mean that winning a challenge can be just ignored. Hand me the keys, now."

"I can't help that I'm amazing." Cole took a step back and shook his head no. "That shit just leaks out of me."

"At least that last statement was true." Jess placed both her hands on her hips. "Damien, tell him that I won fair and square."

Oh, gods. They were like an old married couple. At the very least, they were entertaining.

"She did." Damien shrugged and opened the passenger door. "So give her the damn keys before I decide to eat you."

"Vampire blood is exotic." Cole's face broke into a smirk. "But at least you'd die tasting something better than chocolate."

"You couldn't kill me even if you wanted to." Damien slid into the back seat and shut the door.

"Give her the damn keys." Rage groaned and walked around to the passenger side, opening the back door. He glanced at Cole. "You can ride up there with her. Raven and I will sit in the back with Damien."

"Fine." Cole threw the keys at Jess and pouted. "You better not mess her up."

Jess rolled her eyes and got in the driver's seat while I crawled in the back so I was sitting between Damien and Rage.

There was no telling what would happen in the next couple of hours.

CHAPTER NINETEEN

As soon as we pulled back into the school parking lot, Rage and I were the first ones out. I couldn't believe all of the shenanigans that happened during our trip.

"Did you really have to pour your beer down my shirt?" Jess was still soaking wet from Cole's supposedly accidental fall.

"It wasn't on purpose." Cole grinned as he crawled out from behind the steering wheel. "Unfortunately, it was just too risky to let you drive back. What would've happened if a cop pulled us over and smelled all that on you?"

"I'm full, and I still can't handle this," Damien whispered to Rage and me. "I'm heading back to our place." He moved fast, gaining distance from us.

"You suck." Jess stomped and balled her hands into fists. "You pouted all the way there, and you pulled that stunt. You're just a piss poor loser."

"At least, I'm not the one smelling like piss." Cole arrogantly bobbed his head like that was the best comeback on the planet.

"Okay, it's over." The last thing we needed was Isadora catching wind of this. "Come on, Jess. Let's go back so you can take a shower."

"Fine, but only because you suggested it." She marched past us and headed straight for our dorm room.

"Well, that was fun." Cole chuckled as he watched Jess's dramatic exit.

"You're such a dick." Rage grabbed my hand, tugging me toward the girl's dorm.

"Oh, wow. You acted even worse than that before you shagged your mate." Cole followed behind us.

"Shagged? Really?" What, were we in an Austin Powers movie?

"You must be a pretty damn old vampire." Rage reached over and punched Cole in the side. "Hey, your jealousy is showing."

"Guys, stop." I paused and pointed at Cole. "You need to apologize to her. That was rude."

"Oh, please." Cole straightened his shoulders and crossed his arms. "She got even by telling those hot girls at the next table that I was the worst sex she's ever had." He shuddered. "I'm a great lay."

"I think someone protests a little too much." Rage laughed.

"Aw, Cole." I couldn't help but joke at his expense. He took every opportunity to take a shot at us. "Remember, size doesn't matter. You'll be okay."

"Hey, no." His mouth dropped and he placed a hand over his heart. "I have a big penis."

"Sure, that's what they all say." I reached over to pet his head.

"No." He smacked my hand away and pointed at me. "I can show you."

"You will not be showing my mate your package." Rage lowered his head and glared. "That would end our friendship."

"Ugh." Cole stomped much like a toddler would. "That's not fair and a low blow."

"You know what?" Cole didn't even appear to be attempting to leave, and having him around Jess could lead to even more drama. "Let's go hang out at y'all's place. We never do that."

"I'm sure hanging out is what you mean." Cole winked at me. "But remember vampires have good hearing."

There were no off-limit topics with him. Sometimes, it was mind-blowing.

Rage tugged on my hand. "Jess probably needs to cool down anyway."

"Fine, let's go." Cole took off, grumbling about women.

I CRINGED as I rushed into Professor Shaw's classroom. I had gotten distracted by Rage's lips, and now I was late to class.

He hadn't entered the room yet, so some weight seemed to fall from my shoulders as I slipped into my seat.

"Gah, I was hoping you left school or something." The vampire hissed and scooted her seat farther away from me. "You are a menace, to begin with."

"Now, now." Professor entered the room and obviously heard what she said. "This class will be one of respect for each other, or you'll have to answer to Isadora."

Whispers filled the room. No one wanted to mess with the headmaster.

"Now quiet." He slammed a hand on his desk as he

scowled. "One more interruption, and I'll take matters into my own hands."

The room quieted, and the vampire scowled in my direction.

"Okay, good." He grabbed a marker and headed to the board. "Today we're going to learn a topic that is beginning to get attention and debate. Anyone want to guess what it is?"

"World hunger?" One of the vampires chuckled at his own joke.

"No, not that." Professor Shaw glanced around the class once again. "Anyone else want to take a guess?"

The class remained quiet, and he nodded his head. "Okay, it's the topic of hybrid creatures."

"What's that?" Someone shouted from the back.

"The less technical term is half breeds." Professor Shaw's eyes landed on me.

I hadn't even considered that was a possibility. When I was back home, we only associated with other wolf shifters. My mate was a wolf shifter.

"There are a few people out there who don't respect the ideology that they should only mate, consummate with, or date their own kind. It's a growing epidemic that will have adverse consequences on our society."

"How would it be bad?" The question left my mouth before I could stop it. However, even though the concept was foreign to me, I still needed to understand why it was bad.

"Having two paranormal sides fighting against each other would leave them unbalanced or worse." He sighed and glanced at the ground.

I shuddered at the thought. No one should ever feel

remotely like I had with my wolf. If I had those issues while being only a wolf shifter, I'd hate to put someone in an even worse position.

I RUSHED THROUGH THE WOODS, needing to get to the clearing as fast as possible. Rage had distracted me this morning, which caused the predicament I was in now. Thoughts of his naked body filled my mind, and I lost my footing, stumbling.

Shit, Damien was going to kill me. He was laid back about most things, but tardiness was not tolerated. We'd been practicing combat for the last few months now that my wolf was in control. The flowers bloomed all around, and the air was fragrant like the perfume area of a mall.

When I reached the clearing, there was no Damien though. Just an empty space with grass and some dandelions. There was definitely going to be hell to pay. He'd make sure of it.

I leaned back against a tree, hating that he gave up on me. Sometimes Rage wanted me to be late since Damien had banned him from our training sessions. As soon as something happened and I got hurt, Rage would lose his shit. Now Rage would shift and run on the other side of the woods so I could reach him easily if I needed him.

There was no point moping out here. Might as well turn around and face the music. I pushed off the tree when I heard a rustling behind me. "Damien?" Maybe he was just running late.

Instead of an answer, there was even more rustling of the trees. "I'm sorry I'm late."

Paws began hitting the ground as a large black wolf came into view. Its eyes were locked on me, and it growled, baring its teeth.

I'm surprised he would do this to me, but last time, he'd mentioned that I was getting better. "Are you lost?"

The wolf growled louder and pawed at the ground, growing even more agitated. It began running toward me at full speed.

Not sure what else to do, I shifted into my wolf so we were at least on an even playing field. I growled, knowing I couldn't stand down. Any sign of submission would make it an uneven playing field.

Raven, I just ran into Damien. He told me that you called off training and he was coming to check on you.

The black wolf leapt into the air, and I rolled underneath it, barely escaping its sharp claws. Somehow, knowing that this wasn't one of Damien's training sessions made me nervous.

Are you okay? Rage's voice raised a notch since it was filled with concern.

There's a black wolf attacking me. I didn't have time to chat him up. The wolf was stalking toward me once more.

What do you mean black wolf? Where are you? I could already tell he was running in my direction.

The wolf began to change into human form. Once the black faded into red hair, I knew exactly who it was.

Ashley. It's Ashley.

"Did you really think you'd get away with this?" Ashley's face just about matched the shade of her hair. "Rage will be mine once more when I get through with you, and I'll finally earn my way to the top."

A loud growl ripped through my connection with Rage, and I knew he was going to get pissed when I shut it off.

Still, if I was going to survive this until he got here, I was going to need all my concentration. As I locked down our connection, I felt him fighting the close.

"Are you fucking talking to him right now?" Ashley approached me, and her hands shook with rage. "Stop it. It took three years for them to notice me. You just waltz in here, and in less than a year, you've made it to where I am. That's not acceptable."

Them? It sounded like she was referring to more than just Rage.

Her bones broke as the shift began to overtake her once more. Now I had to at least get a shot in.

I rushed toward her and bit into her arm, holding on tight and fighting against her change.

She growled and rolled over on top of me, making my teeth rip open her skin.

Sensing the perfect opportunity, she went for my neck, but I was able to buck her off before her teeth could sink in.

Not wasting a moment, she charged me again, her eyes revealing her target. She was going for my chest, a fast kill location for a wolf. Damien said the eyes were a tell, and this cemented his lessons in my head.

Within a foot of her reaching me, I lowered my whole body, making her flip over and land on her back.

A bear roared off in the distance, alerting me that both Damien and Rage were on their way. Somehow, my confidence began to kick in.

As she flipped back over onto her feet, her eyes were not only filled with hatred but anger as well. Instead of attacking me face-on, calculatingly, she circled me, taking her time.

I had to be the one who ended this. As I struck her paw,

she turned around and clenched her teeth in my side, using her large canines to tear deeply into my skin.

Her bite burned, and blood began pouring from the wound. I had gotten too confident, and she took full advantage.

A huge smile spread across her snout, and she charged again, aiming for my other side.

If I didn't get a strike in now, it was going to be all over for me. I quickly moved back so her mouth only caught air, and I jumped fast, biting into the back of her neck. I bit hard, hanging on as she tried to buck me off. Her blood poured into my mouth and down her neck.

After a few minutes, she rammed me into a tree, making me lose my grip. The sound of paws crashing through the forest filled my ears. Both Rage and Damien would be here in a matter of seconds.

She must have heard them as well because she hunkered and charged me once more. At the last second, she jumped, aiming straight for my throat.

I stood on my back paws, and my front came down on her once more. This time, my teeth locked into the side of her neck, and I shook my head, making my grasp on her lock.

A whimper escaped her, but I held on tight. At the end of the day, I didn't want to kill her, but if I didn't, she'd come back for me again. Her intent had been clear with this whole set up; she'd planned on killing me. Still, did I want to be like her? When I felt her body weaken, I let go, and she slumped onto the ground.

Rage burst into the clearing with a loud howl. His eyes were completely feral as he took in the scene. When he saw that it was Ashley lying there in a pool of her own blood, his wolf seemed to relax. He walked over to me and nuzzled my head. *You got hurt.*

It's fine. I nuzzled him back, needing him. Since we weren't members of the same pack, we could only mind link in wolf form.

A big grizzly bear entered the clearing, and his eyes went straight to me.

He was worried about you too. Rage licked the spot where I was bleeding.

I just want to go back to the dorm and rest. Today had been one hell of a day, and I wanted it to end now.

Ashely didn't move as she laid soaking in her blood. The only proof she was alive was the beating heart we could all still hear.

Let's get you home. Rage locked eyes with Damien, nodding his head toward Ashley. *Damien can finish the job.*

No, I don't want to stoop to her level. Just because I was here at Bloodshed Academy didn't mean we had to shed more blood than absolutely necessary.

Give me a second. Rage jogged over to Damien, and they did some weird kind of signals.

It was odd that they had their own kind of sign language when they were both in their animal form.

Needing some rest, I laid on the ground, letting the sun hit me. I needed to get to my room and clean my wounds sooner rather than later.

There was some ruffling and then nails tore into my back. Teeth cut into me close to my throat.

A loud growl filled the air as Rage began running toward me, trying to help me. However, my vision was going black. Dammit, if I didn't get her off me now, I was going to die. She started tugging hard, attempting to rip my throat out.

I did the only thing I could do. I stood on my hind legs and pushed back, making her fall underneath me, cushioning my landing. Her teeth let go as she whined in pain.

That bitch was still trying to kill me when she was at death's doorstep. I turned around and sunk my teeth into her neck. She had lost her chance for my mercy. I yanked back, and she began bleeding out.

CHAPTER TWENTY

Isadora paced in front of her dark wooden desk as Damien, Rage, and I sat in her office chairs. She'd been notified by Damien of what had happened. He brought her to the clearing, and when she found the dark black wolf, it was clear she knew who it was immediately.

"How do I explain this to her parents?" Isadora frowned and took a deep breath.

"People know students have died here." Rage shrugged, obviously not upset by what happened in the slightest. "So this shouldn't come as a shock to them."

"Mr. Jackson, I understand that her death was justified." She glanced at the bite marks on my neck. "But handling students' dying is still not the norm."

"Can't we tell them something that would make them proud?" I hated to think of what my parents would do if they received news like this. Honestly, I felt horrible for what I'd done.

"You're wanting her death to be recorded as one of honor?" Damien blinked repeatedly, and his forehead wrinkled. It seemed like he was staring at a ghost instead of me.

"Why not?" I crossed my arms. This wasn't about making Ashley a martyr but about helping her family through a rough time. "Say she protected me from a rogue wolf or something."

"That could work." The headmaster stopped and stared at me. "It would give the school plausible deniability and let her family have peace."

"Rage, do something." Damien shook his head in disbelief. "She was a fucking psycho."

"Look, I'm not happy about it either. Hell, it's partly my fault for leading her on." He stood up from the chair and clenched his hands into fists. "But if that's what Raven wants and the bitch stays dead, then I'll do whatever will make her happy."

"Do you agree, Mr. Weston?" Isadora tapped her foot on the ground. "You're the last one who needs to agree."

"Fine, whatever." Damien stood and nodded. "If that's what Raven wants, I'll go with it."

Isadora startled from his submission, but her neutral expression quickly returned. "Very well. I'll take care of the body. Now you are all dismissed."

Thank the gods it didn't take long. Being around her really gave me the chills.

I followed both Rage and Damien out of the room. When I reached the threshold, Isadora's voice stopped me in my tracks. "Ms. Wright, a word please."

Rage took a step back toward the door, but I held up a finger. "Just give me a moment, please."

"Fine, but I'm staying right here." Rage frowned and leaned against the wall.

"Okay." I shut the door and took a few steps back into the room.

"Never did I imagine that Cole, Damien, or Rage would

allow their hearts to be given to anyone outside their group." Isadora placed a hand on one of the chairs we had just vacated and seemed to try to look through me.

"Well, Rage and I are true mates." Our bond trumped everything.

"I know that, but he's not the only one who loves you."

A coldness ran through my body. "No, you're wrong. They don't love me like that."

"Love is a funny thing." Isadora tilted her head as she examined me, reminding me of the way Professor Shaw had looked at me in class. "Maybe they don't love you the same way Rage does, but they still love you just as much. Somehow, you've gotten the elite three that were unattainable."

"I never meant to …"

She raised a hand out in front of her chest. "I know you didn't mean for it to happen. But let me be clear." Her eyes turned cold, and she scowled in my direction. "You better not cause any more trouble, or it won't be only you that pays."

Her threat was clear, and I refused to show how much it affected me. "Understood." I turned and exited the room.

When I stepped outside, Rage pushed off the wall and growled. "That bitch spelled the room so we couldn't hear."

"It's fine." What I needed at the moment was for him to keep his shit together. There's no telling what he would do if he had heard our conversation.

"Dude, keep it together." Damien punched him in the shoulder. "Let's get out of here before you do something stupid."

I was pretty sure Rage wasn't going to listen, but eventually, he turned, and we walked out of the building.

"What happened back there?" Rage stopped and gently grabbed my hand, turning me toward him.

I didn't want to chance Isadora overhearing us. "Let's go to my room."

"There's my people." Cole strolled out of the cafeteria and grinned. "Do you know how horrible it was to go in there? Those people are fake wannabes. I can't surround myself with that negative energy."

"Dude, can you shut the hell up?" Damien ran a hand through his hair and sighed. "I can't deal with you right now."

"What the hell is wrong with you?" Cole slowly glanced at each one of us before his face turned serious. "What happened?"

"Not here, and not now." I tugged on mine and Rage's joined hands. The four of us together began the trek to the dorm.

When we entered the dorm, we found Jess pacing in the middle of the floor. She sighed when she saw me. "Girl, I was worried. The school just alerted us that Ashley died protecting someone from a rogue wolf, and I knew that shit wasn't true." She ran over to me and threw her arms around me, hugging me hard. "I knew that was bullshit. She's not noble. I was so worried she attacked you."

"I'm fine." My heart sank at what I was going to have to tell her. I hadn't been able to fully process it yet. So I wasn't sure how I felt about my own actions, let alone having to tell Jess. "But she did attack me."

"Whoa. Whoa. Whoa." Cole pulled me from Jess's arms. "That bitch attacked you?" He watched Damien and Rage as they sat on the couch. "Tell me one of you killed her. 'Cause if not, I'm going to bring her back to life so I can kill her."

"No, we didn't." Damien's eyes gleamed with pride.

"Then what happen—" Cole stopped, and his eyes landed on me. "You did it."

I averted his gaze and glanced at my feet. This wasn't something I wanted to talk about.

"Did what?" Jess wasn't processing it as fast as Cole was.

Rage must have known how I was feeling because he came over and wrapped his arm around my waist. "Ashley had dropped a note off at our place for Damien. She told him that she wasn't going to be able to practice with him today and signed it Raven."

"But Raven went to training today." Jess's face somehow turned even a shade paler than normal.

"She was waiting for me." Somehow those words pushed past my lips.

"Wait ..." Jess took a step back and shook her head. "You're saying Ashley attacked you."

"She wanted me dead." That was blatantly clear. What I did was in self-defense, but my stomach turned queasy at what I'd done.

"Raven killed her out of self-defense." Rage pulled me into his chest and ran a hand through my hair. "It was either you or her. Remember that. You didn't go up there to kill her. She intended to kill you."

"Then why the hell did the school make it sound like she was a hero?" Jess's eyes flashed with anger.

"I came up with the idea." She didn't need to blame anyone else but me.

"Why would you do that?" Cole now joined in the conversation. His tone was cold. The one that he reserved for everyone else except those in this room. "Now she sounds like a fucking saint."

"To give her family peace and to give the academy a good story where Bloodshed doesn't look bad." Also, to make myself feel better, but that felt too selfish to admit.

"This can't leave the room." I needed to make sure each one of them understood. "If it does, Isadora will make our life hell."

"She already does." Cole rolled his eyes. "I'm not scared of her though."

"She's not trying now, and she's already a pain in the ass." Damien leaned back and shivered. "Imagine if she actually tried for once."

"If Raven doesn't want us to say anything, then we won't." Rage kissed my forehead and tugged me toward the bathroom. "What you need to do is go take a shower and get some rest. I'll go back and deal with them while you just relax."

I wanted to laugh at those words, but my insides were turning cold. "Okay."

He started the shower and cranked the heat up. "There, it's getting warm." He grabbed my waist and pulled me against him again. "This was not your fault. She chose to attack you. You did it out of self-preservation. You did absolutely nothing wrong. Don't let the guilt eat you alive." He kissed my lips and let go. "I love you."

It was strange because even though I knew that fact, he had never said the words aloud to me until now. "I love you too."

A sweet smile spread across his face, and he opened the bathroom door. "I'll meet you in your room in a few minutes."

Now that I was alone in the bathroom, I turned to see

my reflection in the mirror. Ashley's bite marks were just about gone, and my face was almost as pale as Jess's fae complexion. It was comforting to see that I didn't look any different. There wasn't any darkness clear on my face.

I stepped into the bathroom and let the scalding water try to penetrate my mind's fog. I began washing myself but got lost in my thoughts. I kept reminding myself what I did was the right thing. She wasn't going to stop, not until either she or I was dead. She had let hatred and greed fill her heart.

As I stepped out of the tub and got dressed, it hit me that I would be okay. At the end of the day, I did what had to be done. Although that didn't mean I had to like it or be proud of my actions. There was no right or wrong answer, there was just an answer—one.

There were murmurs in the den. All four of them having hushed conversations, and it was comforting. Every one of them had my back, so I was going to take Rage's advice and get some sleep.

When I entered my bedroom, I didn't even bother turning on the lights. It made no difference to my vision anyway. As I crawled into my bed, something crinkled on my pillow.

I don't remember ever leaving anything there. I grabbed a piece of paper that was folded in half, opening it to see a clear, crisp font forming letters that I had to look over multiple times until it made sense.

Raven,

We've been watching you. Now we know you're Elite material. Our mission is secret, but very important. The very essence of our beliefs centers around improving the vitality of our supernatural society. To do this, we need strong leaders who can make hard decisions. If you decide you'd like to be part of this mission, leave a response at the place you took Ashley's life.

Do not tell anyone, or there will be severe consequences.

-The Elites

My breath caught, and my head seemed to spin. Was this some sort of test by Isadora? I wasn't sure what to do. My eyes became heavy, and I tucked the note between the mattress and box spring. I didn't have to make a decision right now. I just needed sleep.

The End

ABOUT THE AUTHOR

Jen L. Grey is a *USA Today* Bestselling Author who writes Paranormal Romance, Urban Fantasy, and Fantasy genres.

Jen lives in Tennessee with her husband, two daughters, and three miniature Australian Shepherd. Before she began writing, she was an avid reader and enjoyed being involved in the indie community. Her love for books eventually led her to writing. For more information, please visit her website and sign up for her newsletter.

Check out my future projects at my website. www.jenlgrey.com

ALSO BY JEN L. GREY

Bloodshed Academy Trilogy
Year 1
Year 2
Year 3

The Artifact Reaper Series
Reaper: The Beginning
Reaper of Earth
Reaper of Wings
Reaper of Flames
Reaper of Water

Stand Alones
Death's Angel
Rising Alpha

Stones of Amaria (Shared World)
Kingdom of Storms
Kingdom of Shadows
Kingdom of Ruins
Kingdom of Fire

The Pearson Prophecy
Dawning Ascent

Enlightened Ascent

Reigning Ascent

Printed in Great Britain
by Amazon